KIRK

STARGAZER ALIEN MAIL ORDER BRIDES
(BOOK 10)

TASHA BLACK

13TH STORY PRESS

Copyright © 2017 by 13th Story Press All rights reserved. This book or any portion thereof may not be reproduced or used in any manner whatsoever without the express written permission of the publisher except for the use of brief quotations in a book review.

13th Story Press PO Box 506 Swarthmore, PA 19081

13thStoryPress@gmail.com

TASHA BLACK STARTER LIBRARY

Packed with steamy shifters, mischievous magic, billionaire superheroes, and plenty of HEAT, the Tasha Black Starter Library is the perfect way to dive into Tasha's unique brand of Romance with Bite!

Get your FREE books now at TashaBlack.com!

KIRK

1

KATE

Kate Henderson walked slowly through the city park at dawn, the sounds of morning birds twittering in the trees over her head.

The rising sun had turned the sky a lush pink, and a light breeze lifted her hair slightly.

If not for the scent of hot pavement and coffee from a nearby vendor's cart, she might have thought she was really in the woods somewhere, far from the madcap scramble of the summertime city.

Though there were sidewalks in the park, Kate kept to the grassy knolls and hedges. She was unlikely to make it to her destination without being recognized, but there was no point making it easy for fans to spot her.

A sparrow trilled and Kate stopped walking for a moment to listen.

It should have been a perfect morning, but there was something off about the park.

She tried to figure out what. It seemed like a typical summer morning, everything looked the same as usual.

Except that it wasn't.

There were no traffic sounds, no people sounds. There was no rumble of roller skates against the concrete sidewalk, no random baby cries, no acoustic guitars, no jogging shoes slapping a rhythm along the well-used path.

It was early, but the park was always teeming with life.

She made her way cautiously down the embankment to the nearest sidewalk.

It was utterly deserted.

She began to walk faster. Surely someone would be at the plaza in the center of the park. She swore she had just smelled the coffee cart.

But when she reached the plaza it was empty - no coffee vendor, no businesswomen in silk scarves, not even the daily dog walkers - just empty benches and a universe of birds and squirrels enjoying the morning.

Kate felt her the tension drain from her shoulders. She was alone and free. The park was likely shut down to film a movie. She might get yelled at if she bumped into the crew, but the south gate had been open, so she had done nothing wrong.

Just ahead, the path forked. The larger part of the sidewalk forged northward.

But a cobblestone tributary, likely original to the park, meandered off the beaten path and into the rose garden.

Kate had loved the rose garden when she was a kid. Now she seldom went. And if she did, she spent most of her time there answering questions from other garden visitors about her long-canceled TV show.

But this morning might be a chance to visit in solitude.

Kate led a regimented life, there was no built-in down time. If she wandered down that path, it meant skipping an expensive session she'd already paid for with a personal trainer.

You only live once, she told herself in a rare show of determined abandon.

Bucking her sense of duty, Kate turned off the sidewalk and followed the cobblestones toward the garden.

There were sounds coming from the Victorian pavilion that overlooked the sloping garden and the pond below. At first Kate thought it was the skateboarding kids who liked to sit in there, drinking sports drinks and telling dirty jokes.

But when the pavilion came into view she saw it was only a pair of squirrels scolding and chasing each other.

The lush greens and yellows of the park were suddenly a drab backdrop to dozens of blooming rose bushes.

Kate paused and took in the riot of colors and the heavenly scent. Last night's rain had taken its toll on the blooms, leaving a carpet of scarlet and flame-colored petals scattered on the knoll, releasing the blossoms' sweet perfume.

She took it all in hungrily - the roses, the black pond below, the blue sky above. She might never be alone here again, with the city's beauty all to herself.

The thought had no more than formed in her mind before her chest ached with an overwhelming sense of loneliness, though what or who she was lonely for was a mystery. Kate had always been happiest alone.

As if she had called to him, a man appeared on the far side of the garden.

He stood at the curve of the hilltop, his face half in shadow, half illuminated by the rising sun. His dark hair lifted slightly in the breeze. A white t-shirt clung to his muscular form, faded jeans riding low on his narrow hips. He gazed at Kate with steel gray eyes.

Kate gazed back, nearly hypnotized. The breeze seemed to have taken on a life of its own. The warm air swirled around her, feathering her hair across her collarbone in a ticklingly pleasant way.

The petals on the lawn fluttered.

Something lightened in Kate's chest.

The man stepped forward, his gray eyes flashing. He lifted his hands slightly, as if beckoning her.

Kate moved toward him instinctively. She was drawn to him, and it wasn't just his masculine beauty. The dark hair and chiseled jaw were eye-catching, but there was something else, something about this stranger that spoke to her on a molecular level.

The birdsong and squirrel chatter went silent as she drew closer to him, close enough to see the shadow on his jaw, the long, dark lashes that framed those mesmerizing gray eyes.

She stopped when she was close enough to touch him.

He took her hands and smiled down at her kindly.

Kate smiled back, not her professional smile, but a real one, eye-crinkling and spontaneous.

Again, she felt that lightness in her chest, only this time it went all the way down to her toes.

He squeezed her hands and leaned down as if to tell her something.

But movement in her periphery caught Kate's attention. She turned to see what it was.

Rose petals were swirling up off the lawn in the breeze. She watched as they lifted from the emerald grass - scarlet and flame colored petals levitating in slow motion, like rain falling upward.

Kate stared at it, the feeling that something wasn't right tugging at her mind for the second time.

Then it hit her.

There was no breeze now. The air was perfectly still.

Yet the petals still lifted. Thousands of them floated now, hanging in the air like glitter in a snow globe.

"What's happening?" she whispered.

When she turned back to him, he let go of one hand and cupped her face in his palm.

Kate felt her cheeks grow warm.

He fixed his eyes on hers and leaned in, as if he were daring her to pull away.

The flowers were forgotten as Kate waited a split-second eternity for him to kiss her.

A cocky half smile of victory tugged up one corner of his mouth just before he pressed it to hers.

Kate nearly swooned with the rightness of his warm lips against hers, the feel of his strong arms around her.

Desire flooded her body, and Kate tried to go up on her toes to deepen the kiss.

But her feet were no longer touching the ground.

That can't be right...

But she couldn't bring herself to break the kiss to see what was happening. Her body hummed with need. She twined her arms around the stranger's neck.

Faraway bells began to ring. The sound was beautiful at first, but it grew steadily louder and more irksome.

His hard body relaxed around her, the sensation of the kiss fading as the bells jangled louder and louder.

They began to coalesce into a familiar sound.

No, no, no...

But it was too late.

Morning light was already leaking in from the other side of her eyelids. She could feel the cotton comforter wrapped around her.

Kate flapped around for her phone and turned off the alarm.

It was just another regular day.

She sighed and slid out of bed, heading straight for the shower as she tried to imagine what would have brought on that dream. It had seemed so real.

You're tired, Kate. That's all. And you shouldn't have had wine with dinner last night.

But she was embarrassed to feel a sense of loss and longing, not unlike the impossible sadness she sometimes felt at not being able to meet her favorite, now-dead playwrights.

Kate was a no-nonsense person, but her agent inevitably negotiated luxurious housing for her. This condo was a perfect example. The city was gorgeous through floor-to-ceiling windows, but Kate cringed at the thought of what the rental had cost the Comic Con organizers. She'd given up begging Carol to just go for money instead of perks. Carol was convinced that insisting on fancy digs and meals was part of the branding that got Kate higher appearance fees.

And Philly must have been affordable compared to LA, because Kate was in a big enough condo that she had somehow taken on strays.

She knew Cecily from the business, at least. Cecily knew everyone. The chatty make-up artist could probably have had her pick of celebrity condos to crash in. Kate kidded herself that Cecily had chosen her place for the company, but it was more likely that Cecily appreciated Kate's quiet manners and the brunch she cooked on off days.

Beatrix, on the other hand, really was a stray. She was a graphic novelist, which meant she was both wildly talented and continually on the brink of starvation. But her latest series was a breakout, and she'd been at every Con that Kate had attended this year.

When Kate overheard that the girl was Craig's List couch surfing for the summer, it only seemed the decent thing to do was offer her a room in this palace. Of course, there was no guarantee there would be enough space when their little caravan moved on to the next city for the next Con. But Kate had a feeling Carol wouldn't let her down.

She passed Beatrix's room on the way to the bathroom. The door was slightly ajar. Kate could just see the pen and ink drawings taped to the walls, and Beatrix's small form under the covers as she passed. Beatrix wasn't a morning person. If she wasn't up by the time Kate was leaving, Kate would knock on the door to wake her. And Beatrix would groan back grumpily like a hibernating bear. It was their ritual.

Cecily's door was shut when she passed, but Kate knew Cecily had been at the Convention Center painting faces and gluing on scales for hours by now.

Kate opened the door to the bathroom for yet another city view.

The shower really was a senseless thing - all marble tiles with a glass door that must be hell for the maid to keep clean, and a precarious ledge too shallow to balance a real shampoo bottle on. But the water was hot and it felt good to lose herself in the steam.

Kate thrust her hands through her hair, wetting it efficiently.

Dream or no dream, she was going to shake off her mood and do her job today. Being Katie Henderson was a lifelong gig, and there wasn't a stand-in.

2

KATE

Kate Henderson stood behind the table, a winsome smile plastered to her face. Of course, to the fans lined up to meet her, she would always be Katie. She'd gone by that nickname while she was on the show, and in their eyes she would always be little Katie. It didn't help that the character she'd played had also been called Katie. Katie Bly, daughter of the starship captain.

The fans didn't want Kate, they wanted Katie, whether it was Henderson or Bly, so she made sure to look the part. Her long, straw-colored hair almost reached her waist, and the familiar, stretchy uniform of the Starship Inertia clung to her hips, as it had every day that *Suspended in Space* was in production.

Sometimes, when she put on the uniform and looked at herself in the mirror, she felt like the same person she had been ten years ago, when the show was canceled. Other times, she wondered if fans would jeer at an obviously adult woman still masquerading as her teenaged self.

They never did.

The fans were always super pumped. And the one time she'd worn her hair up, there were so many questions that she'd dashed off to the ladies room and taken it down before the signing was done.

"Katie," the woman before her gasped.

"Hi there," Kate said, taking in the woman's full figure, SIS t-shirt, black eyeliner and nose ring.

Was this woman into SIS ironically? That was a thing that had been happening more often lately.

"I need to tell you something," the woman said, leaning in. "You changed my life."

Not ironically, then.

"In Episode fourteen," the woman whispered, "when you kissed the female Wangdoonian, it gave me the strength to come out as bi-sexual."

The Wangdoonian wasn't intended to be male or female. But because of its fuchsia tentacles, a lot of fans had thought it was a girl. And when Katie Bly, daughter of the first mate of the Inertia had consoled the lost alien with a chaste kiss on the top of its round, pale head, viewers had seen what they wanted to see.

"I'm glad the show helped you," Kate told the woman kindly. "*Be yourself—*" she began.

"*—and worlds will follow,*" the woman finished, her eyes sparkling.

Katie reached out and patted the woman's hand. It was pointy as a hedgehog with spiked silver rings, but the blush of pleasure on her face was worth it.

"What's your name?" Kate asked her.

"Jody," the girl said.

Kate wrote *To Jody - Be yourself! Love, Katie* with a flourish and pushed the headshot across the table.

Jody hugged it to her chest and shuffled off.

"Nice," grunted Tex from beside her.

Arthur "Tex" Mulroney had played her dad on the show. He'd made his name in Westerns, but fans loved him as the squinty-eyed first mate on SIS.

Kate shrugged.

"You're better at this than I am," he said with a grin.

"My fan base is a little different," she said, grinning back because she could see what he couldn't - a gaggle of older ladies tittering as they approached him.

"Tex," cried out the first one bravely.

"Aw, hell," Tex grunted to Kate.

But he turned around gamely to greet the women.

Kate figured Tex was pretty happy with how things had turned out. He'd already had a bad back from all the horse tricks by the time he'd arrived on the set of SIS. A show that ran two seasons and then developed a cult following after it was canceled was just right for the middle-aged cowboy. He was a celebrity, but he didn't have to do any more acting. These Cons were a great excuse to stay in nice hotels, meet fans and chat about the good old days.

For Kate, on the other hand, it wasn't so easy. She had always dreamed of acting in films, but after SIS she was permanently typecast as Katie. She'd been unable to land a decent role that fit her three criteria - *no stretch uniform, no outer space, and absolutely no aliens.*

Now, like her character in *Suspended in Space*, her career and life were stuck forever, orbiting the waylaid starship that made her a household name, even after the show was canceled.

After a few years of disappointment, she'd finally packed it in and headed to college. Her plan was to turn her love of real-world astronomy and space into a science education degree and a teaching job. The next generation of students wouldn't know about *Suspended in Space,* and if she cut her hair short enough and started wearing make-up, maybe the parents wouldn't recognize her either. Then she could begin a quiet and organized life as Miss Henderson. Anonymity or not, she'd be making an actual difference in the world, not just trotting around with flowing hair and a tight jumpsuit.

Her agent, Carol, had convinced her to do the Con circuit one last time this summer.

"How do you know you won't change your mind?" the older woman had asked in her trademark unsinkable, happy tone.

"Because I won't," Kate said. "No more space shows. I don't want to play Katie again. And no one wants me to play anything else. My acting days are over."

"Well, just one more circuit, honey, for old time's sake," Carol said firmly. "Then you can hang up that suit for good."

Kate hadn't been able to argue. Carol had been good to her. She'd helped Kate land the role in *Suspended in Space* at a low point in all their lives, when Kate's dad was undergoing cancer treatments. Carol quietly came and picked up Kate to take her to every audition for a year and a half. She had a roster of other clients, but she made time for Kate.

And when Kate finally booked a gig, the pay for *Suspended* was enough to cover her dad's special treatments and even to allow her mother to quit her job in retail and stay home with him to get him back on his feet. Carol's investment in Kate had probably saved her father's life.

So one more tour seemed like a small price to pay.

"Hey there," a familiar voice boomed from the crowd, bringing her back to herself.

At least it had seemed like a small price to pay. Kate had a feeling that might be about to change.

"Yes, it's me," the voice said, drawing closer. "Hi, ladies."

"Shit," Kate said under her breath.

Spencer Carson came into view. He was a hearty male specimen - slicked back blond hair, body bristling with muscles. Objectively, Kate could see how the fans liked him, if you were into that kind of thing.

Unfortunately, Kate knew too much about what was inside that slick blond head to be into Spencer.

He'd had one cameo on the show, as a teenaged alien boy who, for whatever reason, didn't have a ton of alien make-up or a wacky costume. Kate knew the only reason he'd landed the role was because his dad, Barry Carson, was a big-time producer.

Spencer's character had been part of the cliffhanger ending of season one. And his presence had caused a real stir among fans as to whether his character, Prazgar, was intended to become a love interest for Katie Bly.

His presence on set had caused a real stir too. Carson was unable to remember his few lines and continually broke character to laugh or comment. As a result, the powers that be had written him off, and he hadn't even had a farewell at the beginning of season two.

But that didn't stop the fans from dreaming.

And apparently it didn't stop Spencer Carson from dreaming either.

He made his way through the crowd, a look of triumph in his eyes. A black t-shirt with white lettering emblazoned on it stretched across his barrel chest.

Prazgatie 4 ever

PRAZGATIE? She hoped that wasn't really a thing now.

"Move over, old man," he sang out to Tex.

"I don't think so," Tex replied quietly.

"Hey, Katie," Carson crooned. "Miss me?"

Kate studiously ignored him, reaching out a hand to the nearest woman in line and beckoning her over.

"Are you guys a thing?" the woman asked eagerly, looking between Kate and Carson.

"God, no," Kate said.

The woman looked instantly disappointed.

"Wouldn't you like to know?" Carson winked at the woman.

She giggled.

Kate signed a headshot quickly.

"Thanks for coming out," she said, pushing the headshot to the woman.

"I loved the show," the woman said fondly. "You were my favorite, you stood up for yourself."

"Thanks," Kate said. "I was very lucky to be part of the show."

"*Be yourself, and worlds will follow,*" the woman replied fervently and scurried away.

"Okay, break time," one of the organizers shouted.

The fans that were still waiting in the lines sighed their frustration.

"The actors just need a short break," the organizer yelled. "They'll be back in fifteen."

Kate fled to the ladies green room. If she moved fast enough, she could avoid a conversation with Spencer Carson.

Concentric circles in the carpet made the distance to the door at the end of the hall seem farther away.

Kate jogged for freedom and made it inside.

"What is this, *A Hard Day's Night?*" Sadie Stein asked and

then barked out a laugh.

"I'm not running from the fans," Kate told the veteran actress.

"Ah, the co-star then," Sadie nodded sagely.

"I'd hardly call him a co-star," Kate grumbled.

"Don't say that in front of Barry Carson or you'll never work in this town again," Sadie said.

It was probably an exaggeration, but still something Kate had thought about before. Carson could have used his dad's connections to keep her from getting consideration for other roles. It would explain why she had such a hard time landing a new gig after *SIS*. But no one would be that petty.

Would they?

She perched on a chair and slid her cell phone out of her pocket.

KATE:

Why is he here?

CAROL:

Hi there, Katie! Why is who there?

KATE:

Spencer Carson.

CAROL:

What the hell? I told them you would not attend if he was on the panel. Hang tight, Katie-cat, I'm on it.

Kate put the phone in her lap.

Sadie was busy, fluffing up her already very fluffy head of tangerine orange hair. Sadie had to be pushing eighty but she looked fantastic.

Next to her, Kate's reflection looked dull and pasty - a gloomy girl with a hank of blonde hair and a morose expression.

She straightened her posture and relaxed her facial muscles.

"Try some lip liner," Sadie advised, waving a pencil-looking thing at her.

"Katie Bly doesn't wear make-up," Kate said. "Thanks anyway."

"What about in production?" Sadie asked, looking scandalized.

"Oh, *tons* of make-up in production," Kate said. "But it was made to look like she didn't wear any. So they want me au natural for bookings. It's in my contract."

"A word of advice," Sadie offered, meeting Kate's eyes in the mirror. "Never get old."

Kate laughed.

Her phone buzzed.

CAROL:
That son of a bitch isn't on the panel, and they didn't book him. He paid for a ticket.

KATE:
Thanks Carol.

Carol:

I'll have Jeff meet you there. He'll shadow you all day. Sorry to ruin your privacy but I worry about you, kid.

Jeff was an ex-cop Carol had hired as a bodyguard for Kate when Spencer Carson first began to stalk her. Jeff was a nice guy - a little prone to showing off pictures of his grandkids, but Kate didn't mind. She felt better just knowing he was coming.

Spencer had started off friendly enough today. He always did. But he went from sweet to pushy to aggressive very quickly. And Kate was never sure just how far he would go.

A judge had thrown out her request for a restraining order two years ago. And the publicity had been so unpleasant she hadn't wanted to try again, even after Spencer showed up on campus and threatened her last fall.

She had hoped a quiet year meant no more trouble, but she should have known better.

The phone buzzed again.

Carol:

Sorry, Katie, Jeff is at Disney with the family. I already called the company. They're going to get someone else over to you ASAP.

Great.

3

KIRK

Kirk stepped into the enormous hall.

He paused, looking around in wonder. The room was immense - larger than any human shelter he had ever seen

Back on Aerie, Kirk and his brothers floated along the craggy surface of the planet, soaking in starlight for energy. Since their physical forms were gaseous, shelters weren't a point of focus in their lives. They spent most of their time under the stars.

But when radio transmissions from a planet called Earth had arrived, the leaders on Aerie decided to visit their galactic neighbors. And the only way to do that was to take on forms that could tolerate Earth's environment.

The leaders decided that in order to determine whether Earth was friend or foe, a contingent of Aerie's citizens must be sent to Earth. With this in mind, Kirk and his brothers were prepared for the journey. Their gaseous forms were migrated into lab-grown human bodies and they were assigned suitable Earth names, garnered from the selection of Earth media they had consumed.

If the Earthlings accepted these men from Aerie, and the men's experience of human life was positive, then relations between the two planets might begin.

Satisfaction of the full human experience culminated in what some of Kirk's brothers described as a *click,* allowing their soul to become permanently affixed to their human form.

Thus far, the *click* had only been accomplished when a man from Aerie fell in love and mated with a human woman.

But back in the lab in Stargazer, scientists were trying to make the men *click* without love. The attempts were pleasant but led to nothing.

The women who had successfully mated with the first three aliens to arrive grew more and more concerned that the scientists would grow weary of their attempts on their mates' brothers, and ultimately harm the men or the relations between planets.

The women had secretly sent groups of men to different locations, hoping they would find mates and begin a normal human life, far from the reaches of the scientists and the governments of both planets.

Kirk and his brothers, Buck and Solo, had been sent here by his brother Magnum's mate, Rima.

Rima had told Kirk to find her friend, Kate Henderson at the Convention Center. Rima told him she would talk with Kate before he arrived, so that Kate would be ready to help.

Buck and Solo were waiting in the lobby, so as not to draw unwanted attention. It was up to Kirk now to find Kate.

Rima had described Kate's long yellow hair, her dark eyes, and the snug gray uniform with royal blue trim that she would be wearing. He knew he was looking for a table with a logo that said *Suspended in Space*. He expected it would be easy to spot her.

But now that he was here, he understood why Rima had described her friend so carefully.

The room, which was big enough to land a spacecraft in, was crowded with humans of all shapes and sizes. Tables and booths stretched as far as the eye could see, each festooned with logos and labels.

And nearly every woman in his view seemed to be wearing a snug uniform of one kind or another.

Sounds of delight pressed in on him from every direction. And the smell of popcorn filled the air.

"Hey big guy," a man said.

Kirk turned to discover who had called to him. Perhaps this human knew where Kate could be found.

The man was large and smiling. He wore a suit and a pair of dark spectacles, as did his companion beside him.

"Here you go," the man said, handing Kirk a pair of eye coverings. "You're one of us now."

Kirk looked down at the glasses. They were pure black.

"Go ahead, put 'em on," the man said, smiling.

Kirk placed them on his face. To his surprise, he was able to see perfectly well in spite of their dark color, though the room was a bit dimmer than before.

"Sunglasses," he said to himself. He had never seen a pair in real life.

"All you need is a black suit and a memory neuralizer and you can help us hunt aliens," the man's companion said.

"Oh," said Kirk, suddenly afraid that he had been found out.

But the men only laughed.

"Thank you for the sunglasses," Kirk said. "But I have to go find Kate. Do you know her?"

"Kate who?" the first man asked.

"Kate has long yellow hair and dark brown eyes. She is wearing a snug gray jumpsuit with royal blue trim," Kirk recited obligingly. "She is at a table with a logo that says *Suspended in Space.*"

The two men gave each other a look.

"You mean Katie Bly?" the first one asked.

"That's me," squealed a voice from behind.

Kirk turned to see a woman. She did indeed have long yellow hair, and she was wearing a gray jumpsuit with royal blue trim. But something about her seemed off. She didn't look at him the way he expected a friend of Rima's would.

"You are Kate Henderson?" Kirk asked her carefully.

"I'm whoever you want me to be," she said, eyeing him up and winking.

"She's not Kate Henderson, buddy," said the man who had given him the glasses.

"He's right," the woman admitted. "I'm a cosplayer. And Katie is always a crowd-pleasing getup. But I can take you to her line. Do you really know her?"

"I need her," Kirk said.

"Good luck, man," the man told him, clapping him on the back.

The woman who was and was not Kate took his hand and led him through the crowd.

Kirk congratulated himself on his good fortune that he had made a friend who could help, even as he tried to puzzle out why this woman looked so much like Kate. He wondered what a cosplayer was.

They walked past artists making beautiful sketches with colored inks. The drawings looked real but the princesses and dragons were frozen still on the page. Kirk's brother,

Buck, would find it all very interesting. Kirk regretted for a moment that he had come inside alone.

However, Rima had urged Kirk and his brothers to remain discrete.

It had been explained to Kirk on Aerie that his physical form was designed to please and attract human females. But he had not fully understood what power it held until he and his brothers left the lab at Stargazer and entered the world. Women seemed to appear out of nowhere to gaze at them hungrily.

The temptation to explore this heady new power was nearly overwhelming. But Rima had instructed them to find Kate and ask for her help in finding *appropriate* mates. So they had managed the train ride to Philadelphia from Stargazer without allowing the women who prowled after them to find satisfaction.

A woman in a white gown with a round bun on each side of her head gave him a little wave as he passed her stand, which held seemingly endless shelves of t-shirts.

He waved back and she pressed something into his hand.

"May the force be with you," she whispered.

He looked down. It was a black plastic cylinder.

He wanted to stop and ask what it was, but not-Kate was tugging his hand, so he tucked it into the inside pocket of his jacket as they walked.

They passed a jewelry shop and a table where blue colored men with strangely formed ears stood talking.

"Aliens," not-Kate said. "That make-up is some seriously hardcore cosplay."

Make-up was a concept Kirk was familiar with from watching the movies. Did that mean these men were not really aliens? Was this what humans thought of aliens?

But they were rushing past superheroes and Greek gods, artists, and jewelers and more people in gray jumpsuits with royal blue trim.

"Here you go," not-Kate said triumphantly.

"Thank you," Kirk said, looking at the line of people before him.

At the front of the line was a table with a logo on it that said *Suspended in Space*. But there was no Kate Henderson sitting at it.

"She's probably on break," not-Kate suggested. "I hope you get to talk to her. And if things don't work out with her, here's my number."

She slipped him a small piece of paper.

"That's my business card, but my cell number is on there," she told him.

"Thank you," he said. "It was kind of you to help me."

She squeezed his hand and let go, then slipped into the crowd.

He looked down at the card in his hand.

Walker & Stein Pediatrics
Sandra Walker, MD
215-555-0202
Swalkerbabydoctor@walkerstein.com

Kirk had always thought doctors wore white lab coats and carried stethoscopes. But perhaps that was only in the movies. He still had so much to learn.

A man in a navy suit with a badge on a chain around his neck walked down the line, inspecting the people who were waiting.

"Autograph?" he asked Kirk.

"Pardon me?" Kirk asked.

"Are you going to want Miss Henderson's autograph?" the man repeated impatiently.

"No, I'm here to talk with her," Kirk said. "Her friend sent me. She told me she would call to let her know I was coming."

"Oh shit," the man with the badge said. "She's waiting for you. Follow me. You shouldn't have been waiting in line."

Kirk was relieved. They had arrived in the city sooner than expected, but Rima had reached Kate in advance after all, just as she promised.

He followed the badge man through a door in the paneled wall and into a bright hallway. Interlocking circles in the carpet made him feel as if he might be floating.

They reached a door and the man with the badge knocked on it.

"Miss Henderson, the gentleman you were waiting for is here," he called.

"Thanks, Hal," a woman's melodic voice said as the door opened.

Hal nodded to Kirk and headed back down the hallway.

Kirk didn't nod back.

He was gazing in wonder at the most beautiful sight he had ever seen.

Kate Henderson watched him from the doorway, her dark eyes taking him in. Bright light from behind set off her figure, which curved in at her waist and out at her hips in a way that made it difficult for Kirk to think.

"Hey, I'm glad you're here," she said, dragging him inside and closing the door behind them.

"Your friend sent me," he began.

"I know, I know," she said. "My break is almost up but I wanted to fill you in so you know what we're up against."

"I need to speak with you privately though," Kirk said, eyeing the lady who was examining her face in the brightly lit mirror beside them.

"Oh, no, Sadie can be here," Kate said with a smile.

"My instructions were very specific," Kirk told her, shaking his head.

"Don't worry about it, kid. I'm leaving anyway," Sadie said, patting him on the shoulder on her way out.

"Thanks, Sadie," Kate said.

"No worries," Sadie said over her shoulder. "Nice looking guy, they don't make 'em like that anymore. Ha."

Kirk smiled, but he waited until the door was shut behind her before turning to Kate to begin their conversation.

His heart was pounding like an overworked fusion drive. And though he was new to this planet, he was sure he knew the reason why.

Kate Henderson was his mate.

4

KATE

Kate tried hard not to giggle.

Sadie Stein was a woman of a certain age and could get away with calling things as she saw them. But the woman wasn't wrong.

Kate had no idea where Carol had found a bodyguard on such short notice, but she was damned grateful. This one looked more like a stripper cop than an actual security pro. He was tall, lean and muscular with a chiseled jaw and dark hair. The requisite sunglasses and "packing-heat" bulge in his jacket told her he was the real deal. But there certainly wasn't any danger that he would be showing her pictures of his grandchildren.

And there was something... familiar about him. But she couldn't place it.

"Kate, I'm so glad I found you," he said.

His voice was deep, his tone intense enough that she allowed herself to envision him ripping off the sunglasses and taking her in his arms.

She shook her head to clear her thoughts.

"What's your name?" she asked.

"Kirk," he replied.

"Okay, Kirk, here's the story. I'm not at a level of fame where I would normally need help, but there's a guy who's given me some trouble over the years. Did Carol send you a picture?"

Kirk shook his head slowly.

"Okay, then," she said, perching on a stool to slide her phone out of her bag. She swiped at it to find Spencer's headshot. "I'm going to snag his picture for you. He's the only one I'm worried about. The fans can get as close as they want. I don't want you body-checking some kid for trying to hug me, ok?"

"Okay," Kirk echoed softly.

"Here you go," she said, holding out her phone with a picture of Spencer pulled up.

He took the phone from her, then removed his sunglasses to get a better look.

She watched as he appeared to memorize the face on the screen.

When he looked up Kate nearly gasped.

His eyes were steely gray, framed with long, dark lashes.

Her heart began to pound as she realized he could have stepped right out of her dream from last night.

"I am yours," he told her simply. There was something about the way he said it that made her cheeks burn.

"Okay, well, let's get back out there," she said, standing up and hoping he hadn't caught that she was blushing.

"But don't we need to talk?"

"What do we need to talk about?" she asked.

"Your friend said that I should explain everything," he told her solemnly. "She said I should answer your questions."

"There's nothing to explain. You're here to protect me, right?"

The look of consternation was suddenly gone from his face, replaced with an expression so frankly fierce it took her breath away.

"Yes, I'm here to protect you," he told her.

"Then let's do this," she said, heading for the door.

He slid his sunglasses back on and followed.

5

KATE

Kate reentered the convention hall feeling almost giddy.

Kirk walked beside her, forgoing the usual two-steps-behind buffer a bodyguard normally gave her.

Instead of being annoyed by his familiarity, Kate felt immediately safer.

That's not the only thing you feel more of, said the little voice inside her head.

And her inner voice was right, of course. Kirk was handsome. No. He was gorgeous. She would have to be made of iron not to notice.

And in spite of her reputation for pristine professionalism, Kate Henderson was apparently not made of iron.

The crowd began to twitter as soon as they caught sight of her. She smiled at the people in line and headed to her table.

Spencer had made a place for himself at the end of the last table in the row of *Suspended in Space* cast members.

Kirk stayed at her elbow. He was scanning the crowd.

"To my left," Kate murmured to him.

Kirk turned and she knew the moment he spotted Spencer. Kirk's jaw went tight and he clenched his big fists by his sides.

A wave of satisfaction went through Kate.

"Easy, big guy," she teased him. "We're not here to beat him up."

"We're not?" Kirk sounded disappointed.

That was odd. She hadn't pegged him as the sarcastic type.

"Funny," she said. "Nah, just stay close. Hopefully we won't have to interact with him at all."

Kirk frowned, but followed her to the table.

She was a little surprised when he sat down beside her instead of standing against the wall, as was traditional for security. But Tex wasn't back from break yet, so the chair was open, and Kirk's big body effectively blocked her from Spencer's view.

"Thanks," she whispered to him.

"Go ahead, ma'am," yelled one of the line managers to the next woman in line.

The lady came up to Kate, all smiles, dragging a younger woman with her.

"This is my daughter, Samantha," the lady said.

"Hi, I'm Katie," Kate said.

"Hey," the girl said, looking down at her feet.

"Samantha's a big fan," her mom said.

"Do you have a favorite episode, Samantha?" Katie asked, wishing the girl would be allowed to speak for herself.

"Yeah, the one with the Rymple," Samantha said, looking up with sparkling eyes. "Is it true that they filmed you with a dog and then did CG to make the Rymple?"

"Oh, that was one of my favorites too," Kate said. "And no, it wasn't a dog, it was a deer."

"A *deer?*" the girl asked.

"Yes, it was a tame deer," Kate said. "It was the most beautiful thing I've ever seen. They let me feed it before we filmed our scenes together."

"Wow," the girl said, nodding her head up and down. "Righteous."

"So why don't we see you on TV anymore, Katie?" the mother asked.

Because I'm typecast in this same dumb role, or others like it, why do you think? Kate wanted to scream.

Instead she smiled.

"I wanted to take some time out to complete my studies," she said brightly.

"Mom, *God*, do you have to badger her too?" Samantha moaned. "She can do what she wants. She doesn't have to entertain you."

"It's fine Samantha," Kate said smoothly. "I get that question a lot. Thanks for visiting with me. I hope you two have fun at the Con."

She slid a signed headshot to the girl and the two left, arguing quietly.

A group of teenaged boys sidled up to the table next and began asking her detailed questions about the way the ship worked.

Out of the corner of her eye she could see Kirk look over with interest as she did her best to explain the workings of a fictional spacecraft.

The next few hours went on that way. When Tex came back he took a seat further down and Kirk stayed where he was.

Kate noticed her phone buzzing more than usual and

slid the power off between visitors to quiet it. Most likely it was only Carol checking on her and Carol understood that Kate couldn't chat until the signing was over.

At last the line was gone, the last autograph signed, the last question answered.

Kate took a deep breath.

"Is it always like this?" Kirk asked her.

"Yeah," she said. "It's pretty crazy, huh?"

"All those people love you?" he asked.

"That's a funny way to think about it," she mused. "I guess I would say that they all love Katie Bly."

Kirk nodded, but he didn't comment.

Kate wished he would take off the glasses so she could see what he was thinking.

A woman in Katie Bly cosplay walked past and waved, then did a double take.

"Hello, Dr. Walker," Kirk called out.

"Day-um," the woman called back. She shot him a thumbs-up, winked at Kate and disappeared into the crowd.

"What was that about?" Kate asked.

"Oh, she helped me find you," Kirk explained. "She is dressed like you but she is actually a pediatrician. Isn't that interesting?"

"I should be dressing like her," Kate muttered.

"You are dressed like her," Kirk replied, sounding mystified.

Wow, he really was a master of sarcasm.

"Come on," she said. "Let's get out of here."

Kirk walked with her back to the green room. She thought she heard Spencer say something as they headed off, but didn't stick around long enough to find out if he was talking to her.

In the green room, Kirk sat down in front of the mirror

and examined Sadie's many make-up caddies with great interest while Kate slid her phone out of her pocket and powered up.

17 TEXT MESSAGES
 3 missed calls
 2 voice messages

"Oh wow," she murmured.

"Everything okay?" Kirk asked.

Kate scrolled through.

The missed calls, messages and fifteen of the texts were from Rima Bhimani, an old friend she'd met at Space Camp. The two women had been pen pals for a long time, but they hadn't spoken in over a year, so there was no reason for Rima to be desperate to reach her.

Though Kate had thought of her often lately. She'd been really happy for Rima when she read about the aliens coming to Stargazer and Rima falling in love with one of them. It was like a sci-fi novel come true, certainly not Kate's cup of tea, but it was everything Rima wanted in life.

She tapped the text stream.

Rima:

Kate, I know it's been a long time, but I need to talk with you urgently. Can you give me a call as soon as possible?

Rima:

I just tried calling you but it went to voicemail.

Rima:

This is Rima Bhimani, from Space Camp, in case you didn't have my number in your contacts anymore. I'm not a stalker.

Rima:

Oh, god, I read that you have a real stalker, that joke was in really bad taste, I'm so sorry. I wish I could delete that last text.

Rima:

I really need you, Kate. Please call me.

Rima:

I'm sorry, I know I'm bugging you, but this is very, very important.

Rima:

Kate, please, please call me.

It went on like that, but Kate stopped reading and tapped the phone icon to call.

Rima picked up on the first ring.

"Kate," she said, managing to sound hysterical and relieved at the same time.

"Hey, Rima," Kate said. "I was at a signing and my phone was off. Is everything okay?"

"It is now," Rima practically sobbed.

Kate allowed her friend a moment to collect herself.

There was snuffling on the other line, then a little cough.

"Sorry, Kate," Rima said. "Listen, I can't say all I want to say, but the man I sent to see you has a letter that will explain everything. He's... very special to me and I am hoping you can help him and his brothers."

"You sent a man to me?" Kate asked.

"Yes, and his brothers," Rima said. "They should be there very soon. They might even be waiting for you outside the Convention Center."

"And they need my help?" Kate asked. "You know I would do anything to help you, but if they want to break into the acting business literally *anyone* could help them more than I can. I haven't really been working much. I think I might have even been blackballed..."

"No, no, it's nothing like that," Rima said. "These guys just need someone to help them figure out life in the city. They've never been to the city before."

"I see," Kate said, though she didn't.

"Ever since Magnum, I don't know how much I can safely say over the phone," Rima said sadly. "But when they approach you, you'll probably understand right away. And in any case... well... Just read the letter, ok? I'll come out and see you as soon as I can."

"I'll read it, Rima," Kate said. "I wish you could tell me more."

"I should go," Rima said abruptly.

Kate was surprised to hear the dial tone. Rima had always been so polite. And she'd been so anxious to talk.

The phone buzzed again in her hand. It was a text from Carol.

CAROL:

I'm so sorry I wasn't able to get a bodyguard to you in time for the afternoon session. The agency has promised to get someone to you this evening.

KATE LOOKED down at the phone and then back up at Kirk.

"Was that Rima?" Kirk asked.

She nodded slowly.

"But that means that she did not talk with you before," he said, looking surprised. "Did she tell you about the letter?"

She nodded again, speechless.

He stood, his huge, muscular form and undeniable masculine beauty taking on a whole new meaning now that she suspected who he was. *What* he was.

"Here," he said, sliding a letter out of the inside pocket of his blazer, along with a plastic light saber that must have created the lump she'd been sure was a gun or taser.

She reached her hand out.

"The letter is for you," he explained. "This other thing, I'm not sure what it is. A lady with buns gave it to me."

"Thank you," Kate managed to say as she took the letter.

DEAR KATE,

I KNOW we haven't talked in a long time, but I am entrusting you with the safety of the man who gave you this letter, as well as two others, and the safety of my own family. I hope you might find it in your heart to help us.

Kirk

As you know, three aliens from Aerie arrived in Stargazer this fall. My two roommates and I fell in love with them, and as a result, the three men became fully human.

What most people don't know is that my Magnum and his brothers, Bond and Rocky are not the only aliens on Earth right now. There were others, and they are being held in a lab, where scientists are trying to make them click without love. It's not going to work, and I'm afraid of what they will do to these men when they realize it.

I'm also afraid of what they will do to Magnum and me, and the baby we're expecting.

So I've sent Kirk, Buck and Solo to you. (Yes, those really are their names. The only Earth culture they've ever seen is TV and films from the 80s. It's a long story. Kirk can explain.) I hope that you can help them find a safe place to stay, and work to keep them busy.

And I hope you can find them women, kind, decent women to mate with. These men need to find a way to click. The fate of Earth-Aerie relations hangs in the balance.

I don't want to impose on you but there is no one else I know with as big a heart. Or as big a housing budget, if Carol is still your agent.

I will be out to visit you as soon as I can. The boys should arrive at your proverbial doorstep this afternoon. I'm crossing my fingers, eyes and toes that you can help.

Thank you for being my friend.

Love,
    Rima

Kate looked up from the letter.

Kirk stood, looking down at her. His expression of ardent interest suddenly made sense. And so did the innocent comments she had chalked up to sarcasm.

It all made sense.

And at the same time it defied all logic and reason.

"So you're an alien?" she asked him.

He nodded, gray eyes flashing.

"And Rima sent you to me for help?"

"Yes," he said.

"Okay," she said. "Okay, I'll help you."

"Thank you, Kate Henderson," he said. "And I will protect you with my life."

6

KATE

Half an hour later, Kate pressed the elevator button of the condo building and then turned back to Kirk and his brothers.

Though they had all walked back from the Convention Center together, she half-expected to find that they weren't really there, or at least that they weren't such unbelievable physical specimens.

But there they were, just as tall, dark and handsome as they had been before.

The one called Buck grinned at her, his eyes dancing.

Solo's smile was more reserved. He was taller than the other two and quieter.

Kirk wasn't smiling at all. He was gazing at Kate in a way that made her want to blush down to her toes.

Was it true that these guys were here for the sole purpose of mating? She could believe it from the desire that rolled off Kirk's body, sizzling in the space between them.

The elevator dinged, interrupting that dangerous train of thought.

Kate marched in and the men followed.

She pressed the button for the penthouse and the car began to ascend.

The men were so massive that the four of them barely fit in the elevator.

"I like this better than the moving staircase," Solo said.

"But we can't see out," Buck retorted.

"It is more efficient," Solo explained. "It doesn't take up as much space."

"Efficiency isn't everything, brother," Buck teased.

"Thank you for helping us, Kate," Kirk said.

"It's fine," Kate replied, keeping her eyes forward. She didn't dare look up at him for fear of getting lost in his eyes.

Get it together, Kate, she scolded herself.

At last, they reached the top floor.

She launched herself out of the elevator and opened the door to her flat, hands shaking.

"Hey guys," she called out as she stepped inside. "We have company."

"Hey," Beatrix said. She sat on the sectional sofa, sketch board and pencil in hand, as usual. Another pencil was tucked behind her ear. A third was threaded through her ponytail. "Cecily's in the shower."

"Come on in, everyone," Kate said over her shoulder to the guys.

She watched Beatrix's mouth fall open as she took in the new arrivals.

"Beatrix, I want you to meet Kirk, Buck and Solo. They're going to be staying with us for a short while until they can get on their feet in the city," Kate explained.

"Have you been reading my letter to Santa?" Beatrix asked, casting a wide-eyed glance at Kate.

"I know, right?" Kate mouthed back.

"It's very nice to meet you," Buck said, heading right over. "Are you making a drawing?"

"Y-yes," Beatrix said.

He sat on the arm of the sofa, leaning over her with great interest to study the drawing.

"Are you guys hungry?" Kate asked.

"Yes," Kirk said, sounding relieved.

"I'll order us some food," Kate replied.

"Let me cook for you," Solo offered.

"Oh, you don't have to do that," Kate said. "Besides, I don't even know what we have in there. Cecily's the only one of us who cooks and she's been working too much to do it lately."

"It would be my pleasure," Solo said, disappearing into the kitchen.

"Solo enjoys cooking," Kirk explained. "Back at the lab, Dr. Bhimani allowed him to assist in the meal preparation. He has a talent with food."

"Rima's mom," Kate realized out loud.

"Yes," Kirk said. "Dr. Bhimani has taken all of us under her wing, with Rima's help. Do you know her well?"

Kate shook her head.

"Rima took the bus to camp, and I never visited her house, so I haven't met her mother."

"I hope that you will visit Stargazer with me one day," Kirk said. "You can meet her then. When you are able to take time away from your duties, of course."

"That sounds nice," Kate agreed.

Kirk smiled down at her and again she felt a delicious shiver down her spine.

She looked away and noticed Buck and Beatrix talking quietly.

Beatrix was Chinese and rocked a goth style, her petite

frame inevitably draped in shades of black. But somehow she seemed positively tiny, her features even more delicate than usual, in contrast to Buck's enormous frame and broad smile.

Buck grinned down at Beatrix and she actually smiled back. She was normally reserved about people looking at her unfinished work. But she was holding her drawing out slightly so that he could see it better, instead of clutching it to her chest, as she often did when Kate came into the room.

"Your friend is kind?" Kirk asked softly.

He was watching them too.

"Yes," Kate agreed. "She's no picnic first thing in the morning, but she's definitely a good person."

Kirk nodded as if he were satisfied.

"They will be very happy together."

"Whoa," Kate said. "Let's not print up the wedding invitations just yet. You guys are just staying here, until you can get on your feet, nothing more."

"Nothing more?" Kirk echoed. His deep voice carried a note of sorrow.

"Is this to eat?" Solo asked from the doorway of the kitchen. He was holding a glass jar of bright red dishwasher tablets.

"No," Kate said quickly, moving toward him to be sure he didn't try to eat one before she could stop him.

"Oh," he said. "It looked like a dessert. But it smelled like burning."

He handed it over to her obligingly.

Kate made a mental note not to leave anything toxic in an unlabeled container while the men stayed with them.

"I guess I never noticed how delicious those things looked," she said. "Come on, I'll help you in the kitchen."

But Solo was no longer paying attention to Kate.

He stared past her, his blue eyes fixed on the opening bathroom door.

Cecily stood in the threshold wearing only a towel. Fragrant steam billowed out around her.

For a moment Kate saw her friend through Solo's eyes - a wanton angel with auburn curls, blinking back at him with droplets of water still clinging to her lips, the scent of her milk and honey shampoo emanating from her curvy figure.

Kate opened her mouth to explain everything to Cecily, but she got tangled up trying to decide which unasked question to answer first. Why were there three giant men in the apartment? Why was Beatrix showing off an unfinished drawing? Why was she clutching the dishwashing detergent like she was afraid someone would try to take it from her?

But Cecily was too busy gazing back at Solo to ask any questions, or notice Kate's delay.

"We've got company, Cecily," Beatrix yelled from the sofa.

7

KATE

"Why don't I show you guys the room you'll be staying in?" Kate asked.

"Thank you, Kate," Kirk said, motioning to his brothers.

Buck stood. Beatrix looked after him a little sadly.

Solo somehow tore his eyes from Cecily.

Kate headed resolutely to the den on the other side of the apartment where the men would stay.

Though the insidious thought had already occurred to her that Buck and Solo might find themselves in her roommates' bedrooms instead.

The penthouse unit wrapped around the top of the building. The bedrooms were all on the main hall off the entryway. But on the other side of the great room there was a spacious den. It was set up as a TV room but equipped with a set of bunk beds and a pull-out sofa - perfect for their three visitors.

Well, almost perfect.

Kate was crossing her fingers the beds would be big enough to accommodate the hunky giants.

"This building is very tall," Solo remarked as they reached the far end of the living room and the door to the den. He looked out of the floor to ceiling glass without apparent fear.

"Yes," Kate said. "Land in the city is expensive, so architects design the buildings to be as high as possible to get as many homes on one site as they can."

Solo nodded, looking pleased.

"You can see the whole city from up here," Buck said wonderingly.

"The view is another reason they build high," Kate said, opening the door to the den.

"There are curtains you guys can close for privacy if you want," she offered. "And these are bunk beds. Do you know what they are?"

"Yes," Buck said. "We slept in those at the lab."

"Another clever use of space," Solo said approvingly as Buck launched himself heedlessly up the ladder.

"The sofa pulls out," she told Kirk. "And there are extra pillows and blankets in the closet."

Solo immediately went to the closet to check out the extras as Buck opened and closed the blinds on the window by his bunk, fascinated.

It was so odd. Their behavior was so innocent, almost childlike, but their massive bodies were anything but. And the way Kirk had looked at her...

No, they were definitely not innocent.

She turned to find him watching her, one arm braced against the wall.

"Thank you for helping us," he said.

She dared a glance up into those gray eyes.

They smoldered like coals, about to ignite.

"You're welcome," she said. "It's the least I can do."

"It's not the least you could do," Kirk admonished her with a half-smile. "But I will repay you in any way I know how."

Helplessly, Kate pictured him ripping off her clothes, pressing her against the wall and savaging her mouth with torrid kisses.

"Um, it's all good," she murmured. "I'm going to go see about dinner."

He didn't stop her when she dashed out of the room.

She reached the living room with a mild sense of relief, only to realize she'd gone from the frying pan into the fire.

"Kate... Kate, holy crap," Cecily chirped. "Do you know who they are?"

"That's kind of what I wanted to talk to you guys about," Kate said gamely.

"Where did you meet aliens?" Cecily demanded with sparkling eyes.

"*Aliens*?" Beatrix hissed.

"How did you know?" Kate asked Cecily.

"Seriously? Aliens?" Beatrix asked again.

Kate sat on the sofa and the other two perched in their usual seats.

"When I was a kid I went to Space Camp," she began.

"When you were a kid your whole *life* was Space Camp," Cecily teased.

"Yeah, yeah, hilarious," Kate said. "Anyway, most of the kids there were super smart, way smarter than me. But one was super smart *and* super nice. We made friends and we've stayed in touch off and on. Her name is Rima Bhimani—"

"Oh my God, that's how you know aliens," Cecily said.

"Wait, what?" Beatrix asked.

"She's saying that while you were in summer school for drawing comics on your desk, and I was doing nails at my aunt's salon, Kate was at Space Camp," Cecily said. "And her best friend there was Rima Bhimani, the woman who has been all over the news for *marrying an alien*."

"Sorry, I don't memorize every aspect of the news," Beatrix shrugged. "So she's one of the Stargazer wives?"

"Yes, and she sent Kirk and his brothers here to stay with us, until they get on their feet," Kate said.

"Why?" Cecily asked.

Kate bit her lip.

"Come on, out with it," Cecily said in a businesslike way.

"They need to find mates, they have to click with women," Kate said. "If they don't, I'm not sure what will happen - to them, to Rima, to the planet."

"They don't exactly look like they're going to have a hard time with the ladies," Cecily laughed. "Just give them a minute."

"They're on the run," Kate told her. "Rima and her friends busted them out of the lab. The scientists were experimenting on them, trying to get them to click without falling in love."

"How?" Cecily asked.

"I'm, um, not sure," Kate admitted, flushing because she had a pretty good idea of how even though Kirk hadn't explained.

"Kinky," Beatrix said dreamily.

"Focus, Bea," Kate said. "I need to know if you're going to help me."

"You're asking us to mate with them?" Beatrix asked.

"What? No. God, no," Kate replied. "I'm asking you to help me hide them until we figure it out."

"Of course we'll help you, tell us what you need," Cecily said.

Beatrix nodded.

Kate felt tears prickle her eyes.

"Guys, thank you so much," she said.

"Are you kidding? It's only because of you that I'm not living in a lab experiment somewhere," Beatrix said.

Cecily laughed and shoved Beatrix a little.

"Okay, listen," Kate said. "We need to keep them out of trouble. Maybe give them stuff to do here in the apartment while we're at the Con."

"You're not worried about leaving them alone?" Cecily asked.

"It's better than taking them out in public," Kate said.

"I'm not sure about that, Cecily said. "There's a whole slew of people in and out of the building all day. Who knows what they might say or do if they decide to wander down to the lobby? Who knows if you're even allowed to have six people staying in this rental? We don't want to get you busted."

She had a point.

"You think we should bring them with us?" Kate asked. "They'll draw a lot of attention, being so... you know..."

"Hot?" Beatrix suggested.

Kate rolled her eyes.

"I think we can hide them better in plain sight," Cecily said. "And if you keep them close, you can keep them out of danger."

"But you saw it yourself," Kate said. "The moment you laid eyes on them you knew exactly what they were."

"I knew because I saw all three of them at once," Cecily pointed out. "And maybe because I spend a little too much time on trashy websites. So we just don't let them be seen together. We each take one of them with us for the day. All of a sudden, they aren't a trio of aliens, like everyone's been seeing in the news. They're just one hot guy at a time."

It wasn't a bad plan.

"Honestly, I could use some help hauling around my supplies," Cecily added. "And I'm sure Beatrix wouldn't mind the company."

Beatrix winked at Cecily.

"Who knows, maybe they'll find someone to click with after all?"

Kate's heart sank.

"Listen, you can't do that," she said.

"What do you mean?" Beatrix asked.

"You can't just casually date them," Kate said. "And you definitely can't just sleep with them,"

"Why not?"

"Because it's different for them," Kate explained. "I read a lot about this when I saw Rima's story in the news. That click means everything to these men. If it happens it's forever for them - no going back."

There was a moment of silence among the women as they thought about this.

"Is that really so bad, Kate?" Cecily asked softly.

Touché.

Kate hadn't had the best luck with dating. And with Spencer always at her heels, it wasn't worth the hassle of riling him up. Better to wait until her life was settled *far* from the spotlight.

"I'm not really at a good place in my life for dating," Kate admitted. "But even if I were, I wouldn't be dating an alien."

"Why not?" Beatrix demanded. "They're gorgeous and if you're right about the clicking business they're loyal as hell. Where else are you going to find that?"

"I've spent my entire adult life trying to escape the sci-fi lifestyle," Kate said firmly. "I'm not about to marry into it."

Cecily and Beatrix laughed.

But Kate was serious. There were so many reasons for her not to consider a serious relationship right now. But truly, if Kate Henderson married an alien, her whole future would be locked up. There would be no chance to define herself on her own terms, or to dedicate herself to something worthwhile.

And she'd come too far to let go of that goal.

8

KIRK

Kirk walked at Kate's side, trying to take in all of the sights and sounds of the city.

He had never seen so many people all at once. It was thrilling to think that each had their own separate mission to accomplish, yet all worked cooperatively as if they had a shared end - moving and stopping in tandem in response to the colorful lights set on poles that beckoned them and held them off at intervals.

And yet this was no assembly line. There were cries of greeting and honks of car horns that Kate had explained meant the drivers were criticizing each other. Vendors called out to offer cups of steaming coffee.

And beneath it all, Kirk sensed a hidden rhythm to the cacophony, as if the whole city were performing a symphony, but just couldn't decide on a key.

Yesterday, on the way to Kate's apartment, he had been too distracted by the nearness of her small, fragrant body to comprehend anything around them.

But today he felt the weight of his mission to protect her,

so he was determined to assess the world around them in order to be able to note anything out of place.

His observation led to a sense of delight in what he had learned, and he strove to find his own part in the city's concert, even as he scanned the crowd for any threat to his mate.

"We're supposed to meet the bodyguard at the entrance to the hall," Kate said.

"I will protect you," Kirk said. "You do not need an additional guard."

"Oh," she replied. "It's not that I don't appreciate your offer, I do. But professional bodyguards are very experienced. I couldn't ask you to protect me when I know there's a real threat."

"I will protect you anyway," he told her. "You can have as many other guards as you like."

She looked up at him as if assessing his sincerity.

He gave her the same half smile that made her blush yesterday and nearly growled with satisfaction when she flushed again.

As before, she looked away immediately, gazing ahead and picking up her pace.

He hoped that she wasn't confusing his inexperience in Earth customs with innocence. Though he was new to this world of hers, he had lived long enough on his own to understand something of good and evil. He would not allow harm to come to her.

They reached the Convention Center, went through the large lobby and up the moving staircase.

The Con wouldn't start for another hour but there was already a line at the security check-in.

Kirk watched as Kate put her bag through the machine

and stepped through the scanner, then followed through himself.

It was odd how human technology could be so uneven. Solo was often impressed at their ingenuity when it came to engineering efficiency and machines, but Kirk was equally impressed with their guilelessness when it came to their own organic forms. The awkward wand waving was a woefully inaccurate way to scan a human body for weapons, in Kirk's opinion.

But for better or for worse, they were through the checkpoint now.

Kate headed straight for a muscular man who was holding a sign that said *Henderson*.

"Kate Henderson," she said, offering him her hand.

"Mac Reynold," he replied, shaking vigorously. "I'll be your eyes and ears, Miss Henderson. But you'll need to trust me and do as I say. This is a two way street."

Kate's face twisted in displeasure. "I'm not sure what Carol told you, but you're here because of a specific stalker. There is no general security threat."

"That's what they all say," Reynold said with a bitter smile. "But it's my butt on the line if anything happens to you. Which it won't, if you do as I say."

Kirk was not at all happy at the way this man was speaking to Kate. But he restrained himself from speaking for her. Besides, he was focused on keeping a sharp eye out for Spencer.

A young man came out of the checkpoint, his eyes blazing when he saw Kate.

"Miss Henderson, Miss Henderson," he cried, dashing toward her at an astonishing speed.

Kirk stepped between the man and Kate, and took an instant to observe the potential threat.

He was tall but very young. His eyes were flashing, but the corners of his mouth were pulling up with pleasure. He had no weapon that Kirk could see. He wore a black shirt with the letters SIS on it - short for *Suspended in Space.*

He was not a threat. He was just an excited fan.

Before Kirk could point him out to Kate, Reynold barreled toward the boy, some sort of weapon in hand.

"He's not a threat," Kirk called to Reynold.

But the bodyguard had already applied his weapon to the boy, causing him to fall to the ground convulsing in agony.

"Stop that," Kate shrieked. "He's just a fan."

But Reynold put his foot on the boy's chest and did not remove his weapon.

Kirk looked from Kate to Reynold and made a quick decision.

He moved quickly but calmly to the bodyguard, stretched out his consciousness to envelope the man's mass, sensed his weight, and shifted it until it was a fraction of what it normally was. Then he wrapped his arms around the bodyguard's ribcage, and plucked him easily off the boy's chest. He carried him away and put him down against the far wall.

He felt some vestige of guilt at using his gift in public, which Dr. Bhimani had warned him he must never do. But he could not allow harm to come to someone who loved Kate.

"What the hell?" Reynold demanded.

"You have just attacked an innocent civilian, against the wishes of your employer," Kirk informed him sternly.

"He ran up to her," Reynold spat. "I did my job."

"Does she look like she's pleased with what you did?" Kirk asked.

He allowed Reynold enough slack to look over at where Kate sat on the floor next to the boy, who was sitting up.

"I'm so sorry," she said. "Are you okay?"

"F-fine," the kid said. Kirk figured he was embarrassed to admit to being scared in front of his hero. A large dark patch on the front of the boy's pants told another tale. Kirk was glad he did not seem to be badly injured.

"Let's get you some swag," Kate suggested. "I'd like to give you an official Inertia uniform. I'll bet you're the same size as Johnny Santos was when he played 2nd lieutenant Briggs."

"Wow, thanks," the kid said, scrambling up and following her.

"You're dismissed, Reynold," she said over her shoulder as they headed into the main hall together. "Your manager will hear from my agent, and maybe from this young man's lawyer."

"I don't have a lawyer," the boy told Kate as they went into the main hall together.

"This is *your* fault," the disgraced bodyguard snarled as Kirk let him go.

"We have nothing to say to each other. I have to protect Kate now," Kirk said, turning his back on the man and headed after her.

He was betting on the guy being too demoralized to tackle him from behind.

He turned when he got to the door and saw that he had been right. Reynold was walking away, shaking his head.

When Kirk caught up with Kate at her table, she was hugging the boy goodbye.

"Come see me later on for some more swag," she told him. "I want to see you in that uniform."

"Yes, ma'am," the kid grinned back at her before trotting away.

"I'm glad you could cheer him up," Kirk said.

"Yeah, thank you so much for helping out," Kate said. "I don't know what I would have done."

"I guess you'll be calling for a replacement bodyguard now," he suggested.

"No, I think I already have the perfect bodyguard," she said, smiling up at him. "If you still want the job, that is."

Kirk's heart swelled in his chest.

"It would be my privilege," he told her.

But the real privilege was seeing her eyes shine as she looked up at him.

She didn't know yet that she was his mate. But her body was telling him as sure as his own heart told him. They would soon be one.

9

KATE

Kate expected her panic and anger over Reynold's actions to keep her heart racing for hours, but the day went surprisingly well after the morning scare.

She hated to admit it, but Kirk's presence was soothing. The gentle giant was so sweet with her fans.

Tex had messaged her in the morning that his hip was acting up, so his spot was open and Kirk sat right beside her again. As a result, she found herself feeling relaxed and enjoying the fan interactions more than ever, since the spotlight wasn't entirely on her.

"Hey, Katie," a young female fan said, sneaking a glance at Kirk out of the corner of her eye.

"Hi there," Kate said. "What's your name?"

"Bethany," the girl replied with a big grin.

"Nice to meet you, Bethany," Kate said, signing a picture and pushing it toward her. "Did you have a favorite episode?"

"I like the one where you had to figure out whether the Phylorians were good guys or bad guys," Bethany said.

"That was a good one," Kate admitted.

"It was a life-changer for me," Bethany said. "I never really thought about words versus actions like that until your speech."

"That was a great speech," Kate said. "The writers for the show really knocked it out of the park."

"It wasn't just the writers," Bethany said. "You really rocked it, Katie."

"Thanks," Kate said, flushing.

She had always shied away from personal compliments for her performance as Katie. After all, she had been at the audition, seen the waiting room full of other young actresses, any of whom could have played her part and been sitting here right now.

"Say, were you on this show?" Bethany asked Kirk. "I feel like I'd remember."

"No," Kirk replied. "I wasn't on the show, but that is a nice compliment."

"Thanks for coming," Kate said quickly, before he could get into why he was beside her.

"Nice," Bethany said, giving Kate an admiring wink. "He's a keeper."

She disappeared into the crowd before Kate could tell her that Kirk wasn't her boyfriend.

A young couple was already approaching and she turned to them, pulling a headshot off her stack.

And so it went.

A few hours later, Kate was exhausted but happy.

"You're finished?" Kirk asked, looking at the place where the line had been.

She nodded.

"Now what?" he asked.

She looked around. Spencer seemed to have left the

Con, which was great news. Maybe he had finally taken no for an answer.

"Let's do something fun," she suggested to Kirk.

He smiled, eyes crinkling.

"Come on," she said, heading toward the door to the hallway.

Kirk put a protective hand on her shoulder.

A shiver of pleasure tickled its way down her spine at his gentle touch.

She knew she should shrug his hand off before she got too comfortable, but the convention hall was crowded, it made sense for him to stay close, and be sure not to lose her.

When they stepped out into the backstage hallway he removed his hand.

Kate felt a momentary stab of sadness. But she ignored it and moved quickly across the carpet with its concentric circles. They arrived at the green room without bumping into anyone.

"Stay here, I'm just going to change," she told Kirk.

"Okay," he said.

He planted himself in the center of the room with his feet slightly apart, looking as if he might gladly stay there until the convention center crumbled to dust, if she needed him to.

She smiled and scurried into the bathroom with her backpack.

Kate stripped out of the Inertia uniform and slid on a pair of leather jeans, cowgirl boots, a white t-shirt and a purple cardigan.

She looked in the mirror as she twisted her long hair into a bun and pinned it into place like a ballerina.

The bun was smooth and perfect. The face it perched on was utterly ordinary. Kate had nice brown eyes and symmetrical features, but none of them were particularly beautiful. She'd been a cute teenager with baby fat still rounding her cheeks and making her look younger than she was when they cast her as Katie Bly. And the producers had described her look as "approachable". Maybe they figured it would be easy for other girls to put themselves in her shoes - an ordinary girl having extraordinary adventures.

Kate had no argument with her looks. But it was hard not to wonder what Kirk must think of her. Maybe he would like her better if she were a fog or a fine mist or whatever women looked like on Aerie. Or maybe he had learned to appreciate human beauty since watching all those 80s movies to assimilate before his arrival. If that were the case and he compared her beauty to his, she knew she would come out lacking.

Snap out of it, Kate, she scolded herself. *You're not looking for a boyfriend. You're looking for a new life.*

But it was hard not to think about it *a little*.

She pulled on a short purple wig and slid a pair of sunglasses over her eyes, then checked herself out again.

It was a good disguise. Hiding the hair was the key, and covering up the eyes.

She emerged from the bathroom to find Kirk precisely where she had left him.

"Oh," he said, sounding surprised. "What happened to your hair?"

"I'm wearing a wig," she said.

"I see," he said, still sounding confused.

"It's pretend hair," she explained, lifting the wig slightly so he could see her hair underneath.

"Ah," he said. "This is a good disguise. Like the doctor who was disguised as you."

"Exactly," she said. "I'm disguised as a comic book character I like. It's called cosplay. You get to pretend to be someone you admire. Or at least one that looks cool."

"Oh," Kirk said. "This is excellent."

She could see the wheels turning in his head and suddenly wondered what the Con had looked like through his eyes if he hadn't been aware of even that simple concept.

"You can ask me anything you want, Kirk," she said. "If you're confused about anything, just ask."

He opened his mouth, closed it again.

"What is it?" she asked.

"Why do you not wish to have a mate?"

Oh. Not exactly the kind of question she had in mind.

"It's not that I don't wish to have a mate," she said slowly. "It's only that the timing isn't right."

"You are of age," Kirk said. "Your body is ripened."

Kate blushed and bit her lip, trying to think of a way to respond.

"I have said something wrong?" he suggested.

"No," she said. "You're right, my body is mature. It's my... position in life that isn't ready."

"What does that mean?" he asked.

He sounded curious, not resentful.

"I want to get my education, learn to do something that matters in the world - not just be an actress playing the same part all the time," she told him. "I want to help people, make the world a better place."

"So you wish to delay your mating until your studies are complete," he said.

"Yes," she agreed.

"I understand," he told her. "I did not wish to make you uncomfortable by asking you this question. Was it impolite to ask?"

"It would not be polite to ask someone you don't know

well why they aren't married," Kate said. "But since we're friends, it's okay that you asked me."

"Friends," Kirk echoed, in a pleased way. "So what do we do now that you are dressed in your cosplay?"

Kate tried to hide her smile.

"Let's go explore Comic Con," she suggested. "You've spent two days here. You ought to be able to see what it's all about."

"That sounds like a good plan," he said with a smile.

They headed back down the hallway. Though Kirk looked carefully before beckoning her out, Kate still scanned the hall behind her before heading back toward the Con.

So far, so good - Spencer was nowhere to be found.

When they entered the Con, Kirk put his hand between her shoulder blades again.

Kate was surprised to feel the tautness leaving her ribcage. She hadn't even realized she was tense.

They stopped at a booth where a man was making a drawing of a superhero.

Kate watched the shape of a woman appear out of nothing but pencil and paper. Her supple muscle and rippling hair seemed to leap off the page.

"Buck would like this," Kirk murmured.

"This is what Beatrix does," Kate told him.

"Beatrix Li?" the artist asked, looking up from his work.

Kate bit her lip. She shouldn't have said anything that might give her away.

But it was too late.

"Hey, you're—" the artist began to say.

Kate put a finger to her lip, hoping he would get the hint.

"Oh," he said, cutting himself off. "Gotcha."

She smiled gratefully.

"Your drawing is beautiful," Kirk said. "This woman looks so strong."

"Well, she's an alien," the artist explained.

Kirk nodded, the corners of his mouth turning upward slightly.

"Lucky for me, it turns out that aliens are super good-looking and strong," the artist confided. "I guess a lot of guys who bet on blue skin and tentacles are kicking themselves right now."

Kate laughed in spite of herself.

Kirk was cocking his head and looked like he was about to say something.

"We've got to run," she told the artist, grabbing Kirk's hand and heading toward the next booth before he could blurt out anything about gaseous masses and other planets.

"What is *that*?" he asked, looking across the aisle.

She follows his gaze to a booth with a huge three-paneled sign above it:

What-Would-YOU-Look-Like-As-An-ALIEN?

"It's just for fun," she explained. "Want to check it out?"

"Yes," he said, his hand still protectively on her back.

They wandered over to where a guy in a baseball cap was explaining the process to an older lady and her granddaughter.

"You just answer the questionnaire, and then it tells you what type of alien you would be," he said.

"What do you mean *what type of alien*?" the grandmother asked.

"You know, tentacles or wings or whatever," the man

said. "Then I'll take your picture and it will print out with all your alien features. You get to take it home in a frame. It's a good souvenir."

"Oh, Grandma, I want to, I want to," the little girl squealed, tugging her grandmother's shirt.

"Alright, Brooklyn, that seems like a good souvenir," the lady said, smiling indulgently at the girl.

The man handed the girl his iPad and she began swiping at it and giggling.

"Cute," Kate said, looking up at Kirk.

But he was looking intently at something else.

Across the aisle and catty-corner to them was another booth. This one was smaller, with a single panel sign that said simply:

S*targazer* A*liens*

A huge crowd of people was packed around the booth.

Kate moved toward it and Kirk followed.

The display was so simple it almost resembled a high school science fair project. Two tri-fold poster boards were set on a folding table. Blurry printed cell phone pictures were pasted to them with handwritten notes.

The woman inside the booth was speaking - her voice had a touch of regional twang to it.

"... and that's when I knew the man before me wasn't an ordinary shopper," she said in a dramatic whisper. "He was... an alien."

There were sounds of wonder from the crowd.

"But don't they look just like humans?" a man asked.

The woman chuckled and tapped on her display for emphasis.

"I could pick one out from a mile away," she scoffed. "They're not a thing like you and me."

Kirk's hand tensed on Kate's back.

"It's okay," Kate murmured. It was clear to her that the woman was only bluffing.

What wasn't clear was why there were so many people gathered around. There wasn't even a real alien. And People Magazine had a gorgeous shoot with Bond, Rocky, Magnum and their wives just last week with pictures that put the fuzzy ones on the board to shame.

As Kate watched, a girl in a cosplay Inertia uniform leaned against the corner of the booth and gazed dreamily at the pictures on one of the poster boards.

Two older ladies shook their heads in wonder, pointing at the other board and then whispering excitedly to each other.

A teenaged boy elbowed his way into the crowd, drawn to the booth like a moth to the flame.

And then it hit her.

The people at this convention had spent their whole lives stargazing. They had grown up imagining all the stories taking place in a galaxy far, far away.

And now it was here.

Though none of them were likely to go on an outer space adventure, the aliens had come to them. It was nothing short of a miracle.

So they didn't care about the presentation or the showmanship. Just knowing it was all real was enough. And this was more real than any glossy magazine spread.

Watching the crowd, Kate shivered at the thought of

what Kirk's life would be like, even if he did manage to click with a woman and come out of hiding.

He would never have a moment's privacy, not from the paparazzi or even from ordinary people. His image would be plastered on more blog posts and Twitter feeds than anyone could ever read.

The men from Aerie were here. Their lives on Earth were the most amazing sci-fi show that had ever been created.

And it was a show that would never be canceled.

10

KIRK

Kirk watched the people surrounding the booth. It was good to see that they smiled as they looked at the pictures of his brothers, though the lady who ran the booth spoke in a tone that indicated that the men from Aerie were different and dangerous.

Well, she wasn't wrong. They were surely different, though they were trying with all their hearts to assimilate Earth's culture.

And they were horribly dangerous. Not because they were a brutal people, but because the leaders of their planet were watching. If the citizens of Earth came up lacking by his leaders' measurement, they would annihilate this young planet with little effort, and no more regret than -Beatrix had when she tossed an unacceptable sketch into the trash.

"Do you want to leave?" Kate whispered to him.

"Yes," he said.

They turned from the display and headed out toward security.

Kate seemed to understand why he was quiet. She made no attempt to interrupt his thoughts as they moved through security and down the enormous moving staircases to the street.

It was bright outside, and it took a moment for his eyes to adjust. The sun was still high in the sky despite the hour. Dr. Bhimani had explained about the seasons, how summer days seemed to go on and on.

On Aerie this bright afternoon would have seemed dim.

Earth's nearest star seemed to burn in loneliness. She was so far from even this, her satellite. On Aerie, the stars were so close that Kirk felt he could almost touch them.

"I'm sorry you had to see that," Kate said softly. "I hope you won't judge us too harshly."

"What do you mean?" he asked.

"People are... curious," she said carefully. "And we love a good story. That's why the lady said your brothers were different - not because she meant it, only because she knew it would build dramatic tension. Do you understand?"

"I do," he said. "But she was right. Maybe not about being able to spot us, but we are different, though we try not to be. Does that frighten you?"

He liked that she didn't answer right away, politely denying her fear without thinking.

Instead she bit her lip.

"No," she said at last. "I'm not frightened of you at all. I've trusted you from the moment I met you, even before I knew. I think I'm afraid *for* you though. Afraid of what could happen to you here."

"I'm not as innocent as I may seem," he told her.

His brothers had warned him that their lack of familiarity with Earth's customs, combined with their overall good-naturedness, would cause many humans to view them as innocent or even child-like. Indeed, most people he interacted with seemed to forget all about the fact that he came from a race that had mastered intergalactic travel long before the first human walked the Earth.

Kirk found it endearing.

She looked up at him for a moment, and he wondered what she would ask him.

But movement ahead of them took his attention.

Spencer Carson walked toward them on the sidewalk.

The man's face was twisted into an ugly scowl, fists clenched at his sides. He was definitely a threat.

"Kate," Kirk murmured, stopping and placing a hand in front of her to hold her back while he assessed the situation.

"Katie Bly," Spencer drawled.

"That's not my name," Kate said in a clear, firm voice.

"I don't know who your new guard dog is, but you can tell him to heel," Spencer said. "I can walk you home from here."

"I don't want you to walk me home," Kate said.

"That's not what you said before," Spencer said. "*I don't want to be alone. Walk with me, please.*"

"Those were lines in a script," Kate said wearily. "It wasn't real, Spencer. We were actors."

"We might have been on a TV show, but we weren't acting and you know it," Spencer said angrily. "There was a connection between us, and I know you felt it too. I don't understand why you're playing hard to get. But it stops now."

Kirk had heard enough.

"Spencer Carson, it is time for you to leave," he said in a tone that was calm but firm.

Spencer looked up at him, eyebrows lifted slightly as if in surprise, as if he had forgotten Kirk's existence.

"Fuck you," Spencer said. His voice was pitched a bit higher than before.

"Miss Henderson does not wish to speak with you," Kirk informed him, although it seemed to him that she had made her wishes perfectly clear. "It's time for you to move on."

"You can't tell me what to do," Spencer shrieked.

"Please just go," Kate said softly, breaking Kirk's heart with the note of hopelessness in her tone.

Spencer stepped forward, reaching for Kate.

Everything seemed to happen in slow motion after that.

Kirk blocked Spencer's arms, pinning them down against his body.

Then he reached out with his mind to envelope the man's mass. It was distasteful to stretch his consciousness around someone like Spencer Carson, to take him in. But it was a necessity.

Kirk used his innate ability and reduced Spencer's weight to something more manageable, then wrapped his arms around the man and lifted him as if he were a pile of clothing. He moved Spencer out of their way and set him down beside the marble wall of the nearest building.

Once again he called on his gift, this time slamming it down in reverse.

"Don't come near Kate again," he whispered to Spencer.

"Wh-what did you do to me?" Spencer moaned, going down on one knee under his newly increased weight.

"Leave her alone," Kirk repeated, and pushed down just a little harder for emphasis before returning the man to his original heaviness.

He turned to Kate.

She stood on the sidewalk a few feet away, her mouth forming a tiny o.

"Are you okay?" Kirk asked her.

She nodded.

"Let's go home," he said gently.

She nodded and they began to walk.

Kirk snuck a peek over his shoulder and saw that Spencer was leaning against the wall, an odd look on his face.

Though he hoped the scare he'd given the man had been enough, Kirk was glad Kate was walking quickly. The shock of the experience would wear off soon and he didn't want her anywhere near Spencer when that happened.

"Thank you," Kate said.

"You're welcome," he told her. "It is my job."

"You're very strong," she noted. "I'm glad you could subdue him without hurting him."

He nodded.

"Not because I like him," she said quickly. "Only because I don't want you to hurt anyone on my account."

"I don't want to hurt anyone at all," Kirk said, smiling down at her.

Kate was an amazing person. She had been hunted and harassed by this man, yet her desire to protect Kirk from felling guilt was greater than her wish for her own safety. There was not a hint of petty vengeance in her. Kate was pure and kind.

A perfect mate.

"What are you thinking?" she asked.

"Only that I admire you," he told her.

"Well, I admire you too," she declared. Then she blushed pink for the third time in a day.

"I love when you do that," he told her.

"What?"

"I love when you blush."

Her cheeks grew rosier still and he had to restrain himself from bending to brush them with his lips.

"Here we are," she said.

So much for his alertness. They had reached the apartment without him even noticing.

He had never been one to let his guard down so easily.

But then, he had never met anyone as damned distracting as Kate Henderson.

11

KATE

Kate walked quickly to the elevator. She needed a bit of space from Kirk, just for a moment, to calm her mind.

And her body...

You're coursing with adrenaline from the confrontation with Spencer, she told herself sternly. *You're not really attracted to that massive alien.*

But she was. Oh, she was.

She pushed the button for the elevator and it sang out immediately, doors sliding open.

She stepped in and Kirk followed.

It was only as the doors slid closed that it hit her that they were alone in the tiny space.

She looked away, but he was reflected back at her in the brass wainscoting of the elevator's walls - a hundred Kirks standing sure and tall beside her.

He moved and she held her breath, waiting for his touch.

But he was only leaning over to push the button for their floor.

"I forgot," she muttered.

"You had a busy day," he said gruffly.

He was so close. His masculine scent enveloped her, and she could practically feel the heat pouring off him.

When the elevator dinged to announce their arrival she nearly jumped.

"Here we are," he said.

He followed her to the door, which she opened quickly.

"Why don't you have a seat, I'm just going to change out of this stuff," she suggested.

"I'll make us a snack," he said.

She headed down the hall, grinning like a fool, and determined to change clothes quickly before he ate something that wasn't food.

Kate removed the wig, let down her hair, and stripped down to her underwear. She went to her bed to grab the t-shirt and jeans she'd set aside for this evening.

But what she saw on the bed made her gasp.

"Kirk," she called out, her voice thin and reedy.

"Kate?" Kirk's voice traveled to her from down the hallway. "Kate is everything okay?" he called, getting closer.

She looked down at the bed. A thousand flame colored roses covered her sheets. The note in the center of the garden of loose blossoms was written in thick black ink:

ALL THE PRETTY *flowers and cruel thorns make me think of you, my love.*

I'll be back tonight so you can thank me in person.

-S

KIRK STEPPED into the room and she collapsed into his arms.

"Kate?" he breathed, wrapping his arms around her instinctively. "Oh."

"He was in here, he was *in here*," she whimpered into his chest.

She felt like a baby. This wasn't like her. Kate was independent, strong, and resourceful. But this was like a living nightmare.

"It's time to call the police," Kirk said.

"We can't," she replied.

"Of course we can," he said. "He was on your property without your permission. He left you a creepy note."

"See? Even *you* know that's creepy," Kate declared. "And you're an alien."

"So do you want me to call for you?" Kirk asked.

"Wait," Kate said. "Wait, wait, wait. Let's just think this through. If we call the police, they might or might not believe it was Spencer. They might or might not do anything about it. But one thing will definitely happen."

"What's that?"

"It will definitely make the news," she said. "They'll search the apartment and find evidence that Bea and Cecily and I aren't the only ones living here. They'll ask you and your brothers questions you can't answer. Plus, my uncle is the captain of a nearby police precinct. If he gets wind of anything going on involving my name, he will definitely blow it way out of proportion."

"Maybe you can call him for advice."

"I haven't talked to him in years," Kate admitted. "To be honest, he's kind of a jerk."

"Well, you can't put yourself in danger just to protect me," Kirk said.

"I may not be in danger," she replied. "Think for a minute. We just saw Spencer on our way here. He was coming from the opposite direction. That means that he had already done this when you put him in his place. Maybe he wouldn't have done it at all if he'd had that, um, conversation with you first."

Kirk was quiet. She hoped he was giving it some thought.

"Meanwhile, I can try to find out how he got in by asking the security guard in the morning," she went on quickly. "Alvin can look at the key fob log and the footage from the lobby. That way we can make sure it doesn't happen again."

"I don't like it," Kirk said.

"I don't really like it either," she admitted. "But I like it better than the other options."

He went silent and she noticed his arms were still around her, the unconscious movement of his hand between her shoulder blades soothing her.

"I'll go along with this under one condition," Kirk said at last.

"What is it?"

"You are not to be out of my sight," he said. "Not for one minute."

"I'll need bathroom breaks," she protested.

"You can have them with the door open," he allowed.

"I'll have to sleep," she said.

"I'll sleep in the chair," he said, indicating her reading chair in the corner.

She bit her lip. Normally, she'd be outraged at the implication that she couldn't take care of herself. But there was something about being close to Kirk that made her feel safer than she ever had on her own.

"If you're on the fence about this arrangement, I'm glad," he told her. "Because then we can call the police and my brothers and I will just have to find another living arrangement."

"No," she said quickly. "No police. You can trail me like a duckling if it makes you feel better."

She felt him smile against the top of her head.

"Yes, I will trail you," he agreed.

12

KIRK

Kirk held Kate to his chest.

Though he was concerned about the man who had frightened her, it was hard to concentrate with his mate warm and soft in his arms.

Kate had removed nearly all of her clothing and he could feel her smooth skin under his hands, and the tickle of the frothy looking fabric that covered her breasts.

The delicate scent of her reminded him of the wild flowers near the pond back in Stargazer.

His body was responding to hers in spite of the circumstances. He hoped she would not be offended. This was new territory for him.

Kate moved slightly and he prepared for her to pull away.

Instead she nuzzled his chest, sending lightning bolts of need through him.

"Kate," he murmured in warning.

But when she looked up at him all he could think of was how beautiful her brown eyes were. How sweet the curve of her cheek.

He slid a hand up her back to touch her face and she closed her eyes and leaned into his palm.

The temptation to brush her cheek with his lips hit him again.

This time, he didn't resist it.

In the back of his mind a thousand warnings sounded, reminding him that she had just had a scare, that she had said she didn't want a mate.

But none of them could compete with her sigh of pleasure as his lips caressed her skin.

"Kate," he said again, wanting to warn her, but unable to remember any of the words of this language but her name.

She took it as an invitation instead, and opened her eyes, gazing up at him with some nameless emotion he hoped was the beginning of love, then pressed her lips to his.

Fireworks went off behind his lids and some ancient knowledge ingrained into his human form took over, thumbing her jaw open, pressing her against him possessively, tasting the honey sweetness of her tongue.

Kate whimpered against his mouth and pressed herself closer still, as if she couldn't get close enough.

A storm was raging inside Kirk, a beast clawing to be set free.

He fought his impatience and kissed her slowly, carefully, like the men in the movies. She was precious to him, and so delicate.

She trembled in his arms, slid her hand up his arm and threaded her fingers in his hair.

The slight pain mixed with the pounding desire was almost too much for him.

He walked her backwards to the bed.

"Wait," she whispered, pulling away.

He nearly screamed with frustration, but saw that she had let him go only to sweep the flowers off the bed.

When there were only a few petals remaining, she crawled in.

Kirk's mouth watered as she tantalized him with the movements of her round posterior. His cock yearned with a mind of its own, craving her heat.

But when she lay back on the bed and opened her arms to him it was his heart that truly ached.

He waited an instant, wishing he could memorize her soft expression of need, the curve of her outstretched arms, the creaminess of her thighs. The way she looked at him as if he were the only man in the universe.

Then his need pressed down on him with a force he was powerless to lighten. He crawled on top of her, inhaling her scent, pressing himself against her heat.

Kate moaned and clawed at his t-shirt.

He sat up on his knees and pulled it off for her.

"Oh," she whispered, looking at his chest as if he were a sparkling gift.

He grinned. He was glad she liked this body he had been given. It was meant to bring her pleasure and he saw now that its design was effective.

But Kirk wanted to bring her pleasure on his own merits.

He lowered himself over her again, praying for control over the screaming demands of his own body so that he could attend to hers.

Kate kissed him again, nipping and sucking on his lower lip in a way that he could feel in his groin.

He pulled away, afraid of how those attentions would end, and nuzzled her neck.

She gasped and arched her back, offering up her beautiful breasts, frustratingly encased in tickling swirls of lace.

He kissed his way down to them, sliding his finger between her breasts to find the clasp.

"Like this," she whispered, sliding her hand between her own breasts, releasing it.

He peeled the garment away.

Her breasts were beautiful orbs, soft and pale with dark nipples crinkling and pouting.

He had been shown filmed copulations in the lab in Stargazer. These movies were supposed to help him satisfy his own member and possibly click into his human form without the aid of a mate. The films had been interesting, and he had stimulated himself to many culminations. But nothing in those films had prepared him for this.

Nothing could have readied him for the feel of her beneath him, the feast laid out for his senses, the responsibility of satisfying the need he knew she felt.

She clenched her thighs around his hips and his cock throbbed in sympathy.

He lowered his head and nuzzled one of her perfect breasts.

"Oh," she whimpered.

He licked one ruby nipple into his mouth, worked it with his tongue, sucking lightly.

Kate bucked her hips up against him.

The pleasure was dizzying.

He lavished her other nipple with attention, licking and sucking, as he slid his hand over to the other one, to stroke and tease her.

"Oh," she whimpered again.

"Hush, my love," he whispered against her ribcage as he moved down her body. "I know what you need."

He rubbed his rough jaw against the softness of her stomach.

She giggled and he smiled as he pressed kisses against her belly button.

When he reached the lace of her underthings he waited, not wanting to do anything she didn't want.

But Kate slid her thumbs under the waistband and dragged them downward.

He was struck with the image of her pleasuring herself as he had done in the lab, those delicate fingers sliding into her own warmth, and he had to close his eyes and breathe deeply to avoid losing control.

Kate lifted her bottom and he slid her panties off, flung them to the floor.

Kate lay back, her golden hair spread on the pillow, her dark eyes filled with need.

Kirk drank in the sight of her, then lowered his head to press kisses against her inner thigh.

She allowed her legs to fall open slightly and he followed the curve of her thigh, hypnotized by her irresistible scent.

13

KATE

Kate clenched the sheets in her hands, feeling like she might actually die of anticipation.

It wasn't that she was inexperienced. But this was something different. Kirk was focused, so focused on her, that she thought she might fly apart before he even touched her.

He pressed his lips to her sex and she saw stars.

She cried out shamelessly, and he rewarded her with a slow stroke of his tongue against her opening.

She whimpered and tried not to lift her hips up to his mouth for more.

"Mmm," he hummed against her clit.

Her hips quivered and the room began to fade before her eyes. There was nothing, no apartment, no city, no universe - only the leisurely movements of his tongue against her sex.

He licked and stroked her slowly and carefully, seeming to refine his movement based on the whimpers and cries that he wrenched out of her with his teasing, but never giving her release.

When she thought she couldn't bear any more, he pressed a finger against her opening.

Kate moaned.

"Is that good, my love?" he asked her tenderly.

"Yes, yes, yes," she whimpered.

He lowered his head again and licked her right on her throbbing clitoris.

Kate cried out helplessly.

She could feel him smile against her thigh.

He licked her again, moving his finger inside her gently.

Kate lifted her hips, pressing herself wantonly against his mouth, wordlessly begging for more, more, more. She had never felt so frantic, so desperate.

Kirk responded immediately, licking her clit into his mouth, sucking lightly and stroking it with his tongue, all the while moving his finger gently inside her.

Pleasure coiled inside her like a spring. Kate cried out and felt herself exploding with ecstasy.

Her body spasmed and she arched off the bed slightly, but Kirk held her down firmly, working her with his mouth and hands, extending her rapture until she couldn't take any more.

When the last tremor had faded, he crawled up to lie beside her.

"That was... amazing," Kate whispered to him.

"Yes, it was," he whispered into her hair.

He stretched out on his back and pulled her on top of him.

She smiled and slid a hand down his upper arm. He was so muscular it defied reason.

She let her hand slide lower, against the ridges of his abs.

Kirk wrapped a hand around her wrist, pinned it to his chest instead.

"That's enough for tonight," he told her. "You should rest now."

"But don't you want—?" she began.

"Of course I want that," he said, his voice tight. "But it's not the right time."

"Why not?"

"Kate," he said, then paused. "Kate, I know you don't want a mate right now. I'm afraid that if we make love, I will click with you. And there is no going back after that."

"Oh," she said, surprised.

"I have chosen you as my mate," he told her casually.

"Wait, what?"

"That doesn't require anything of you, darling," he told her. "That's about me. And it's done. I didn't have to say the words. It's been true since the moment we met."

She leaned her head against his chest, felt him brush his lips across her hair.

"If you don't want me around, it will be difficult, but I'll be able to leave. On the other hand," he went on, "if I were to *click* with you, I might not be able to help myself."

"Oh," she said, again, trying to get her head around it.

"And you already have one stalker too many," he joked.

"You would never be like him," she told him earnestly.

"I would never put myself in that position, my love," he told her. "Sleep now."

She wanted to argue, to ask him questions.

But the slow beat of his heart under her ear and the movement of his hand across her shoulder blades lulled her into sleep.

14

SPENCER

Spencer Carson sat on the edge of his seat. It was a nice office chair with a leather seat pad and an ergonomically adjustable base. His dad had bought it for him when he began to realize just how much time Spencer was spending in front of the computer.

Spencer never leaned back though. He always sat on the edge, the metal frame of the chair cutting slightly into the backs of his thighs.

On the screen in front of him, Katie Bly spoke to him in an endless loop.

"We're friends, Prazgar. That means something special to me," she told him, her voice slightly husky.

She was sylphlike in the video.

Katie had gotten heavier since then, but Spencer loved her anyway. Even though he himself had made every effort to be fit and attractive for her - more attractive than the reedy boy he had been on the show.

"Thank you, Katie," young Spencer said on the screen.

"I don't want to be alone. Walk with me, please," Katie Bly begged. A close-up showed her large, frightened eyes.

At least those were the same.

He pictured her as she had been when they filmed the scene, his palms sweaty, her smile encouraging.

He pictured her the way she was when he'd seen her earlier that night, the same large frightened eyes as in the scene. She was asking him to go and to stay at the same time. Fucking Katie.

And then that guy she was with, that bodyguard, he had *done* something to Spencer.

Spencer had no idea what the hell had happened, but one minute he'd been ready to rumble, and the next his body was weighted to the ground, unable to move.

And it wasn't any kind of sick martial arts move. Spencer knew about those, since he'd studied them all. Online, mostly.

No, it was something else, something suspicious. The guy must have had a weapon he'd somehow kept hidden. Maybe he'd zapped him with it on a pressure point or something, but there was no way he'd done what he did with just his bare hands.

To cheer himself up, Spencer pictured Katie after that, going home to find his gift.

He'd been tempted to bury himself in her sheets and wait there for her, surrounded by the flowers, but he knew better.

Not yet, Spencer, he told himself. *Build her anticipation. Women love that shit.*

"*We're friends, Prazgar. That means something special to me,*" Katie told him from the screen.

"It means something special to me too, baby," he told her.

The phone rang. It was the private eye he'd hired to keep an eye on Kate.

"Hey," Spencer said.

"She's home," the man said.

"And?" Spencer hoped the guy didn't want a fucking bonus for pointing out the obvious.

"It's the bodyguard," the man said. "He didn't leave."

"What?" Spencer asked.

"The bodyguard is still there," the guy repeated.

Spencer hung up.

"*Fuck*," he yelled.

He had known something was up with the bodyguard.

He hadn't expected that Katie was sleeping with him.

"*I don't want to be alone. Walk with me, please,*" Katie pleaded from the screen.

"Whore," he replied, slamming his laptop closed.

It was time to get serious. The bodyguard did not belong in the equation. He was not supposed to spend time with Katie. He was going to ruin everything.

And there was something else... something weird about him that Spencer couldn't quite put his finger on.

"Spencer, everything okay?" his mom called from the hallway, sounding tired.

"Fine," he yelled back.

Everything *was* going to be fine.

Spencer was going to get to the bottom of it for sure.

15

KATE

Kate woke up loose-limbed and happy.

At first she thought the warmth in her chest was because of the sun dawning pink behind the city skyline, filling her room with soft light.

Then she remembered.

Oh, Kate, how could you? her inner critic scolded.

But she wasn't really sorry.

She eased herself over slowly only to find that Kirk wasn't in bed with her anymore.

But his side of the bed was still warm and sounds carried into the room from the hallway. She must have awoken when he shut the door.

She slipped out of bed like a ninja, freshened up in the attached powder room, slipped on a robe and went to find him.

She didn't have to go far. The sound of singing came from the kitchen.

Kate padded down the hallway and turned the corner to see a surprisingly domestic sight.

Kirk, wearing nothing but pajama bottoms, was dancing

around the kitchen, singing along to the radio. He held a frying pan in one hand and a kitchen towel in the other. His muscular torso was lightly dusted with what she hoped was flour.

The song on the radio was early Cyndi Lauper. The station must have been doing an eighties throw-back weekend. Kirk had a surprising command of the lyrics.

His dance moves weren't exactly slick, but his body was hot enough to make up for it.

She watched, agog, as the pajama bottoms slid a little lower on his hips.

"Kate," he exclaimed. "I am making pancakes."

"I can see that," she said, though she also saw that the ingredients that were mostly spilled on the countertop. "Can I help?"

"That would be wonderful," he said, with feeling. "I have learned about pancakes from watching the movie *Uncle Buck*, but you do not have a snow shovel, so I am only making small pancakes."

"I like to make small pancakes too," Kate said, trying to hide her smile. "Let's see if we can get everything organized."

They worked together for a few minutes. Though they had been intensely physical last night, Kate found herself feeling self-conscious all over again about the spark that passed between them every time their fingers brushed.

At last the batter was ready and the pan was hot.

Kate poured a perfect circle of batter into the center of the pan and handed Kirk the spatula.

"When you see bubbles all the way to the middle, then it's time to flip it over," she told him.

"Thank you for helping me," he said.

"Thank you for making breakfast for me," she said. "That was very nice of you."

"I want to learn to do all things done on Earth," Kirk said dreamily.

"Like what?" Kate asked, wondering what he thought Earth people did all day.

"I want to prepare delicious food, of course," he said. "I want to learn to drive a car - and to wash and maintain it too. I want to travel and explore this planet, read books, listen to music, and learn everything about my new culture."

An idea began to take root in Kate's imagination. It was a picture of this simple, quiet private life that Kirk wanted, a life that bore great resemblance to the life she herself wanted to live.

"Have I said something offensive?" he asked, his brow furrowed.

"No, not at all," Kate said. "I was just thinking."

"Ah," he said. "The bubbles are in the middle."

"Slide the spatula under it and flip it over," Kate said. "It's time."

Kirk slid the spatula under the pancake smoothly. He flicked his wrist enthusiastically.

The pancake flew two feet into the air and landed miraculously back on the pan with a slap.

Drips of batter splattered out onto Kate.

She squealed.

"Oh no," Kirk said. "Are you okay?"

"I'm fine," she said, wiping batter from her cheek. "You've got a strong flipping hand."

Kirk smiled and leaned in to help her clean up. He wiped his thumb across her forehead, then her other cheek.

Kate felt her body melt at his nearness.

"Oh, there's some on your lip," he murmured.

But instead of thumbing it away, he leaned down and licked her lower lip.

Kate held her breath.

He licked her lip again, slowly, before pressing his mouth to hers.

Kate forgot the mess, the pancakes, the whole world around her. There was nothing but Kirk's arms around her, the taste of his lips, the pulse of her need for him.

He pressed her against the counter, his kisses a demand.

Kate moaned and slid her hands up his bare chest.

"I think something's burning in here," Cecily's voice said from the hallway. "Oh."

Kate managed to pull away from Kirk's kiss.

Both her roommates and his brothers peeked in the doorway to the kitchen, various expressions of amusement and surprise on their faces.

"I am learning to make pancakes," Kirk told them, his arms still around Kate.

"I don't think that's how you do it," Beatrix quipped.

Cecily gave her a gentle shove in the ribs.

"Beatrix is right," Solo said from the doorway. "You don't even have a snow shovel."

16

KIRK

Kirk smiled at his brothers, who were observing him with envy.

"Were you guys out all night?" Kate asked.

She had pulled away from his kiss, but he noticed that she hadn't let go of his hand. She was embarrassed to have been kissing him, but she wasn't ashamed of the bond they had formed.

This was very promising.

"I think that's burning," Cecily said, pointing at the pancake.

Kate let go of his hand to pull the pan off the stove.

"We were at a party," Buck said happily.

"What party?" Kate asked.

"A graphic novelist from the UK," Beatrix said. "The party was wild, He hung his hotel room with sheets of butcher paper and by the time we left the whole place was covered in drawings."

Kirk looked to Buck, who shook his head slightly.

Kirk was glad his brother hadn't displayed his gift. Each

of the men seemed to have an enhancement of some kind, an echo of their strengths back on Aerie.

But Dr. Bhimani had cautioned them not to use their gifts in public.

Buck had followed that advice. Kirk only wished he could say the same. It was risky for him to use his power on Spencer, but Kate was in danger. If he had another chance, he would do it again.

"So now what?" Cecily asked.

"I think these pancakes are a lost cause," Kate said. "Sorry, Kirk. Do you guys want to go to the diner around the corner?"

Kirk wasn't disappointed. As long as she wanted to spend her time with him, he was happy.

He noticed how Beatrix stole a glance at Buck before nodding her head.

Kirk hoped that they were bonding too. It seemed almost too perfect that they had met these three amazing women. If only they were receptive and compatible, he and his brothers could spend their Earth lives together with these three who were almost like sisters.

Though he wanted to immerse himself in his new planet's culture, Kirk found it easier to do so when he had his brothers around to help him figure it out.

And secretly he worried about Solo, whose stern personality hadn't softened even after months on this lush and welcoming planet. Solo would need Kirk and Buck to help him adjust.

"The diner sounds great," Cecily said.

"Agreed," Solo assented.

"Let me get my stuff," Kate said.

She disappeared down the hallway.

"We should change too," Cecily said to Beatrix.

Beatrix nodded and the two headed down the hallway.

Kirk began to clean up the kitchen. It was harder than he had expected.

"Let me help you, brother," Buck said.

He grabbed a towel and began sweeping the dry ingredients from the counter into his hand and then dumping it into the trashcan.

Solo leaned against the wall, apparently deep in thought.

"You mated, didn't you?" Buck asked quietly.

"No," Kirk said, shaking his head. "But we will. I can feel it."

"That is good," Buck said, clapping Kirk so hard on the back that he nearly stumbled.

"How are things with Beatrix?" Kirk asked.

"I'm not sure," Buck said thoughtfully.

"She seems to like you a lot," Kirk said.

"I thought so," Buck said. "But she has declared that she will not take a mate. She is mated to her career."

"How is this possible?" Kirk was stupefied.

"I think it's a figure of speech," Solo said from his post in the doorway. "It means that the time she would devote to a family is now devoted to her work."

"Ah," Kirk said. That made sense. Though it was terrible news for Buck.

"If she means this, why does she seem to like you?" Kirk asked.

"Cecily took pity on him and explained it," Solo said. "What Beatrix is doing is playing at liking Buck. It's called flirting. Beatrix is very skilled at it."

She certainly was. So skilled that Kirk wasn't sure this could be the case. No one could be so precise at feigning attraction, could they?

He remembered that Kate's job was a form of pretending for entertainment. Could she be pretending with him?

He thought of their time together last night. If she was pretending, she was truly gifted at it.

"This place is very confusing," Buck said sadly.

Buck was usually the most optimistic of the brothers. Seeing him in pain stung Kirk.

"She will come around, brother," he told Buck. "I think this flirting may only be practicing for something more."

Buck's expression lightened at this.

"Here they come," Solo breathed.

Kirk heard movement in the hallway. Beatrix appeared first, followed by Cecily.

At last Kate joined them. She was wearing her wig and sunglasses again.

"I don't want to be recognized while we're out," she explained.

She looked very beautiful no matter what she wore, but Kirk found her especially interesting to look at with the purple wig on. She looked like herself and not like herself at the same time.

They headed out of the apartment to the elevator, everyone chatting at once.

It was hard to remember his formal duties while in the midst of this friendly group. But he managed to check the elevator before they got on.

It was hardly big enough to hold all six of them. Kate wound up pressed against him in a very pleasant way. He watched sadly as the digital floor display counted down, not knowing when he would feel this closeness with her again.

He tried very hard not to think about getting in bed with her again, though the flashes of last night invaded his consciousness every few seconds - the scent of her, the sound of her moans, the movement of her hair as she thrashed out her pleasure.

Easy, Kirk, easy.

When they reached the bottom floor he scanned the lobby before stepping aside to let everyone off.

He took Kate's hand as they headed for the lobby door and she squeezed his back.

Sunlight bounced off the water in the lobby fountain and the rich scent of coffee drifted in the air. Everyone coming and going looked as cheerful as he felt.

Kirk wondered if his own happiness had somehow expanded to embrace them all, infusing them with the delicate joy of the beginning of his bonding with Kate.

17

KATE

Kate relished the feeling of the sun on her cheeks and the heat of Kirk's hand around hers.

The sidewalks of Philadelphia were filled with young and old and everyone seemed to be smiling, as if they could feel her happiness.

Kirk was focused on the world around them, eyes scanning the crowd for any sign of danger, even as he stroked her knuckle with his thumb.

She wondered if he realized how good he was at his job. He'd held it for less than twenty-four hours, yet he was one of the best bodyguards she'd ever had.

Beatrix and Buck were leading the way, chatting about someone they had met at the party the night before. Bea looked happy, her rare smile lighting up her face again and again.

"What are you thinking about?" Cecily asked.

"Just thinking it's nice to see Bea in such a good mood before noon," Kate said.

"Why?" Solo asked.

"Beatrix is not a morning person," Kate explained. "She doesn't like to wake up."

"She didn't wake up," Solo pointed out.

He had a point.

Cecily laughed. "Solo, you're hilarious," she said, patting him on the arm and turning back to Kate.

Solo blinked in a pleased way and glanced down at the place Cecily had patted.

Buck opened the door to the diner and Beatrix swept in, the others following. The host seated them in a large booth and wandered away to find a waitress. Kirk picked up a menu and paged through it with an expression of wonder.

"All of these foods are made in this place?" he asked.

Kate nodded.

"That is impossible," he said.

"The part of the restaurant that we can see is less than half the size of the place," she explained. "Below us there's a basement full of freezers and refrigerators with ingredients. In the room behind this one there are rows of ovens and cook tops as big as this table. And there are dozens of people working back there too."

"This is very clever," Kirk said. "The restaurant gives the appearance of leisure, yet hard work is being done just out of sight."

"I never thought of it that way, but yes, I guess that's true," Kate allowed.

"Hi there," a waitress chirped. "What can I bring you all to drink? Oh wow."

That last was in response to the three hot guys at the table.

Kate realized belatedly that they had gotten careless and brought the boys out in public together. Hopefully the crowd at the diner wasn't as alien-crazy as the one at Comic Con.

Cecily took over ordering for the table as the waitress managed to stop ogling the boys long enough to write everything down. At last she tottered away.

"She was checking you out," Beatrix said to Buck.

"You are jealous," Solo observed, looking from Beatrix to his brother and back.

"No, I'm not," Beatrix retorted.

"She is," Solo told Cecily.

"Yeah, but it's bad manners to notice," Cecily told him.

"My apologies," Solo said very politely to Beatrix.

Bea looked like steam might come out her ears.

"There is no need for you to feel jealous of this waitress woman," Buck remarked, grinning at her. "I will gladly tell you what I would like to eat whenever you wish."

Beatrix started to scowl at him, but it finished as a smile. It was as if her own face had betrayed her by echoing his expression.

Bea had it bad.

Kate was glad. Bea needed to let loose and connect with people. Buck was good for her. He might get her nose out of her comic books for a change.

The waitress came back to cover the table in coffee cups. Another waitress had joined her. She was helping to carry the mugs of coffee, but Kate suspected she was there more to check out the view.

When her eyes slid down Kirk's body, Kate felt herself stiffening in affront.

But the big alien didn't seem to notice. Or if he did, he gave no indication as he ignored both waitresses and turned to Kate, pressing a kiss to her cheek.

All better.

Her phone buzzed in her pocket and she slid it out to check.

1 text message

Carol:

I saw PopWire today. Your little secret is out. Or maybe I should say your "big" secret. LOL. Now I get why you didn't want another bodyguard. You go, girl! (But next time, please inform me so we can get out in front of it and milk it for PR!)

"What the heck?" Kate muttered.

Kate:
What are you talking about?

Carol:
Oh shit, you didn't see it. PopWire - front page, you won't miss it.

Kate clicked the link. She didn't even have to scroll down.

Who is the mystery man with Katie Henderson?

THERE WERE pictures of her at the Con, sitting beside Kirk, taken with a cell phone.

It wasn't so bad. Nothing had happened between them in public She could still play him off as just a bodyguard. She scrolled through them quickly.

Then she hit the last photo.

In the picture Kate was smiling at a fan, and patting Kirk's hand.

Kirk gazed at Kate, a slight smile tugging up the sides of his lips, his gray eyes rapturous under the long lashes.

He wasn't looking at her as a client, or a colleague or even a friend.

No, Kirk was gazing at Kate with a naked expression of love. His feelings were as clear as if he had written her a sonnet and posted it on a billboard.

Kate's stomach dropped to her feet.

"Is everything okay?" Cecily asked.

"Kate?" Kirk whispered, touching her hand.

She turned her phone off quickly and slipped out of the booth.

"I-I need to go," she muttered.

"Kate," Cecily said.

"Just look at *PopWire*," she said. "And then get these guys separated. It's only a matter of time before someone figures out who they are."

"Wait," Kirk called out.

She dashed out of the diner and onto the street where the sun suddenly seemed too bright and the heartless pedestrians too cheerful.

18

KIRK

Kirk leapt out of the booth and ran after Kate. He had no idea what was wrong, but he had obviously been remiss.

More than once.

As a bodyguard, he had allowed his charge to become vulnerable in the street.

And as her friend and future mate, he had failed to be the confidante she chose in her moment of distress.

He burst out of the door and onto the sidewalk. His shoulders went down in relief when he saw her small figure advancing into the crowd. He'd been afraid he might lose her out here.

"Kate," he called to her.

She didn't slow down.

"Pardon me," he said as he pressed his way through the crowded sidewalk. "Excuse me."

On Aerie, this abandonment of basic good manners would have been tantamount to social suicide, but here there was little resistance. Not that it mattered - he would have gladly lost his reputation to find and protect her.

At last he caught up to Kate. She was walking quickly, purple hair of her wig bouncing on her shoulders, her mouth set in a narrow line.

"Kate," he said. "I'm sorry you are upset. Have I done something wrong?"

"You haven't done anything," she said. But she didn't look at him.

"I can tell that something is wrong, how can I help you?" he asked.

She stopped, took a deep breath and then sighed it out.

"Come here," she said, sliding her phone out of her pocket.

They walked over to the side of a building, allowing the pedestrian traffic to pass them by.

She held up her screen.

On it was a picture of Kirk looking at her. It was a lovely picture. Kate was smiling kindly at a fan. Kirk remembered her as a young woman who had been empowered by Kate's role in the television show.

When he first put on the body he now wore, Kirk had felt it was excessive and clumsy.

But this photograph showed him its fine delicacy. He admired the way the curve of his lips and the sparkle in his eyes were the perfect mute expression of the love and longing he felt for his mate. If he had not learned her language this picture would still have shown her everything she needed to know about his feelings and his intentions.

"It's lovely," he told her. "Who took it?"

"I don't know," she said. "But it's been published online in a gossip column."

"Oh," Kirk said, trying to follow.

"That means that the fans will be trying to figure out who you are," she explained. "And you don't have a backstory for them to find. And you're big and gorgeous. Which means they're going to put it together that you're an alien. Especially if they see you with your brothers."

"Oh," Kirk said, his heart dropping.

"What can we do?" he asked.

"You have to go away," she told him.

"I won't leave you."

"You can't stay, Kirk," she said. "You see what's happening. It's only a matter of time."

"I don't care what happens," he said calmly. "I won't leave you. It is my duty to protect you."

"I can get another bodyguard," she said.

It wasn't the same, and they both knew it. He paused, hoping she would acknowledge this.

"Kirk, this could put you and your brothers at risk," she said. "And it will end my dream of having a life outside of the world of science fiction."

"*This* will end your dreams?" he asked, looking back down at the photograph and thinking how strange it was that their dreams could be so at odds.

"Yes," Kate replied, placing her hand on his.

He handed her back the phone.

"I can't leave you without protection," he told her. "I'll stay with you until someone else comes."

"And then what?" she asked.

"My brothers and I can leave immediately," he said.

"Don't do that," she told him. "You can stay with me until you figure out what's next."

"We will not impose on you," he said. "We can find other lodgings quickly once you have protection."

She swallowed hard.

He wished he could see her eyes. But her expression was impenetrable behind the dark sunglasses.

She began tapping into her cell phone so quickly he wondered if she could be forming actual words.

A moment later it buzzed back at her and she nodded, satisfied.

"Shall we?" he asked, indicating the sidewalk.

But her phone buzzed again.

She looked down at it and smiled.

"Perfect," she cried, looking greatly relieved.

"What is it?" he asked. Surely the manager couldn't have found another bodyguard so quickly.

"Cecily says that Solo will act as my bodyguard today," she said. "You can help her at her booth. That way we won't be seen together again."

It was a smart plan. But it still stung to hear her excited about it.

"Guys," a familiar voice shouted from behind them.

The others had caught up.

"Thanks so much," Kate said to Solo immediately. "I really appreciate your help."

"It is my pleasure," Solo said stiffly.

Jealousy exploded through Kirk's chest like a wind storm on Aerie in the bright star season. He had never experienced such an emotion. It felt like he was dying.

And Solo did not care for Kate. Kirk should not feel jealous.

Kirk was perplexed by both the intensity and irrationality of his feelings.

He watched as Solo accompanied Kate down the sidewalk, Cecily and Beatrix following and whispering animatedly.

"This is difficult for you, brother," Buck said, putting an arm over Kirk's shoulder in a friendly way.

"Yes," Kirk agreed.

"But she is your mate," Buck said.

"I am not sure that she will ever believe it," Kirk admitted.

A woman walking the other direction did a double take at the sight of them.

Buck winked at her.

Kirk elbowed him.

"What?" Buck asked. "We were built to bring them joy."

"Now that I have tasted jealousy I would not wish it on Beatrix," Kirk grumbled.

"Perhaps a little jealousy would do her good," Buck said with a grin.

"You can't mean that," Kirk said.

"If the movies have taught me anything about women, it's that you have three choices when it comes to making things right with them," Buck said.

"I'm listening," Kirk said.

"Number one - they love flowers," Buck said.

Kirk thought of Spencer's flowers and shuddered.

"I don't think that's always true," he said. "What else?"

"Number two - make them jealous," Buck said. "If another woman notices your good qualities maybe she will too."

That was unacceptable to Kirk.

"And number three?" he asked.

"Ah, that's the hard one," Buck said, shaking his head. "Number three is giving them space."

"Like what we traveled through to get here?"

"No, brother. Not like that." Buck said with grin. Kirk didn't see what could possibly be funny.

"Like a room or an apartment, then?" Kirk asked. He did not know how much space cost, but he was sure he could not afford anything nearly as luxurious as what she had already.

"No, no, like space between you," Buck explained. "Removing yourself from the situation and letting her have time alone to sit in front of a rainy window and think things through. And hoping that she decides that she would be better off with you than without."

"That *is* difficult," Kirk allowed.

He thought about what Kate had just told him.

What she was asking for was exactly this - space, distance between them - the one thing that would hurt him most.

But if she asked it, it was imperative that he give it to her. If he didn't, he was no better than Spencer Carson.

And as much as he resented Solo sharing time with her, he knew his brother would keep her safe.

"I will give her space," he said.

"Oh, my brother," Buck said sympathetically, squeezing his arm around him more tightly. "I will try to help you pass the time."

They had arrived at the Convention Center.

Kate looked over her shoulder at him before going inside with Solo. Kirk imagined that her eyes were sad, even though he couldn't see them.

His heart ached, but he only nodded at her and watched her disappear. He had no wish to make this any harder for her.

19

KATE

Kate entered the convention center feeling unmoored.

Solo walked beside her, eyes roving over the crowds as if he expected someone to try to pick her off at any moment. Somehow, his vigilance was not as comforting as having Kirk by her side, even though he still turned as many heads.

On paper, Solo was exceptionally handsome with his cool expression and long, lean body.

But he lacked Kirk's dancing gray eyes and the warm smile that made him out-of-the-ball-park gorgeous to Kate.

Chin up, you're doing the right thing, her inner businesswoman said.

But it didn't feel right.

She buttoned her lip and made her way through security with Solo.

"Now what?" Solo asked as they entered the main hall.

"I've got to go to the green room and change into my costume," Kate said.

He nodded and stayed close as she slipped past the

booths and out into the hallway with the circles on the carpet.

"This carpet is nonsensical," Solo said.

"What do you mean?" she asked.

"Patterns in floor coverings often signify social status, tell the story of a great cultural myth, or even offer building directions," Solo pointed out. "This pattern is nothing but meaningless shapes."

"I never thought of that," Kate said.

"Neither did the person who designed the hallway," Solo scoffed.

They continued to the green room without further conversation. Kate changed clothes and they made their way back down the hallway to the main hall in silence. Just before they reached the door, Solo paused.

"I hope I did not cause offense with my remarks about the carpet," he said.

"What? Oh. No, not at all," Kate said.

"I'm a bit on edge," he said.

"I'm so sorry," she replied. "I don't think Spencer would actually attack physically."

"No, it's not that," Solo said, looking uncharacteristically uncomfortable. "It's Cecily. I... I don't feel right being far from her."

Wow. Kate had picked up on the vibe between Beatrix and Buck, but she'd had no idea that Solo and Cecily were bonding.

"I'm so sorry," she told him.

"No, it's fine," he said at once. "Everything is as it must be. I am happy to know you better."

"That's so sweet," Kate said, feeling suddenly sympathetic to her formal new friend. "I'm happy to know you better too. Now let's get in there and greet some fans."

Kirk 123

The meet and greet got underway, and she made it through the day without anything unusual happening.

Spencer never showed up, and although that should have made her feel better, it left her with an off-center feeling of anticipation all day, like arm hair lifting before a lightning strike.

On the other hand, the more hours that passed without seeing Kirk, the more she felt an impending sense of loss.

The fans were great though, helping to pull her out of herself.

When one or two asked about her boyfriend, she'd simply said she wasn't seeing anyone. And although there were some raised eyebrows, no one argued.

Solo stood behind her, in a proper bodyguard manner. During their breaks, he gave her space in the green room while the other women who came in and out flirted with him shamelessly.

To Solo's credit, he did not seem to even notice their advances, but rather engaged with them in an earnest and polite way that made it easier for Kate to understand why Cecily was becoming fond of him.

Solo offered to accompany her someplace for lunch, but he looked relieved when she told him she wanted to rest and urged him to go check in on Cecily.

"Just for a few minutes on the way back from retrieving our meals," he assured her.

"Take your time," she told him. "I'll probably just nap."

But as soon as he left, Beatrix arrived with two paper cones of bright pink cotton candy.

"Where's Buck?" Kate asked.

"What the hell?" Beatrix said. "I hang out with the guy for like twenty-four hours and now we're supposed to be joined at the hip?"

"Sorry, I didn't mean..." Kate wavered.

"Kidding," Beatrix said. "I'm totally messing with you. He's having fun out there. When I saw Solo go past I thought I'd sneak in here and see how you were doing. Any trouble today?"

"Spencer doesn't seem to be here, if that's what you mean," Kate said.

"It's not, but that's good news," Bea said.

"Fans are asking about the guy from the pictures, but they're not giving me any grief when I say he was a bodyguard," Kate said.

"Good." Beatrix nodded.

"You're here to see if I'm okay about Kirk, huh?" Kate asked.

"Houston, we have lift-off," Bea said with a smile.

Kate pulled off a tuft of cotton candy and put it in her mouth. The sweetness melted away in an instant.

"I thought it was just an attraction," Kate said. "But I kind of miss him today."

"Yeah?" Beatrix asked, popping a big fluff of cotton candy in her mouth.

"How's he doing out there?" Kate asked.

Beatrix shrugged. "Cecily is trying to keep him entertained. Her minions are flirting with him to beat the band. But he's got kind of a hangdog look."

Kate felt a little guilty about the relief that surged through her.

"I'm sorry to hear that," she said. "But I know I'm doing the right thing - for both of us. He can't get found out, or he'll bring trouble on his whole family. And any hope I have of leaving *Suspended in Space* behind would be over if I were publicly dating an alien."

"I've never understood that," Bea said thoughtfully.

"What?" Kate asked.

"Most actors would trade anything to be a household name," Bea said. "Why do you want to leave it behind so badly?"

"Because I want to make a difference," Kate said. "I don't want the world to see me as a gawky teenager forever."

Bea shrugged and plucked off another tuft of cotton candy.

"Have you heard from the studio yet?" Kate asked, eager to change the subject.

"Yeah," Beatrix said glumly.

"What now?" Kate asked.

Beatrix's break-out graphic novel had been a hair's breadth away from a movie deal for months. But the studio always seemed to want one more assurance that it would be a success.

"I got the investors they wanted," Bea said. "Now they want a star attached."

"Isn't casting their job?" Kate asked.

"You would think so," Beatrix said. "But I'm learning that nothing in Hollywood is that easy. They want a star behind it and one who is willing to work for SAG minimum to make it happen."

There was a tap on the door.

"Kate, it is me, Solo," came a loud whisper. "Are you awake?"

Beatrix snickered.

Kate elbowed her.

"Come in," she called to Solo.

"I've gotta go before Buck gets into trouble," Beatrix said. "Text me if you need anything."

"Thanks, Bea," Kate said, wrapping her arms around her roommate in an impulsive hug.

Bea hugged her back, then quickly scooted out the door as Solo was coming in.

"I'll tell Kirk you said 'hi'," Beatrix called over her shoulder as the door shut behind her.

Kate shook her head. She didn't want to encourage Kirk, but there was something nice about knowing Bea would try and cheer him up.

"I did not know enough of your dietary habits to discern which you would choose." Solo said, laying out wax paper packages along the make-up counter. "So I brought eight sandwiches for you to examine."

"If anything ever happens to Carol, I'll know who to call in for the celebrity treatment," Kate said with a smile.

"I do not know what this means," Solo replied.

"It means thank you for the sandwiches," Kate told him gently. "I'm glad you're here."

20

KIRK

Kirk sat obediently at Cecily's booth while she ran to grab lunch.

The items in the booth were very interesting. Cecily made masks and prosthetic attachments that could transform a human into all manner of fantastical creature, from a fairy to a zombie, or even an alien - although the human imagining of aliens was unlike anything Kirk had ever encountered.

Her makeup area held bowls of tiny scales and shimmering jewels in addition to pots of creams and potions in every color imaginable.

A display of photographs hung along the back of the booth. Most were black and white shots of actors wearing her creations. He had asked her why the photographs weren't in color when her creations certainly were, and she had shrugged and told him it was tradition.

He hadn't had time to ask many more questions. The booth was busy nearly every moment, either with fans wanting to buy a signed copy of her memoir *Make-up Sex,* or with actors from different films and televisions shows she had worked on stopping by to visit.

Kirk had discussed human behavior with Dr. Bhimani back at the lab. He was fascinated by how differently the people of Earth interacted with their world.

By Dr. Bhimani's estimation, he was pretty sure Kate would be described as an introvert, in spite of the fact that she spent so much time interacting with so many people.

Cecily, on the other hand, seemed to grow more energetic the more people she talked with. The Con didn't seem to exhaust her the way it did Kate - instead, it appeared to fuel her.

Kirk admired her extrovert strength, but secretly preferred Kate's quieter demeanor, which was more like his own.

The day passed slowly, as every woman's smile made him think of Kate. He missed her horribly, which made little sense as he had only met her a few days before.

He was amazed to find that his sadness was not merely a state of mind, but also a physical affliction, causing him a tightness in his chest and a hollow feeling in his stomach.

Though he had felt moments of regret on Aerie, he had never felt this way, turned inside out with grief, and he wondered if the emotions were part of the physical body.

Inwardly though, he knew it wasn't true.

He had chosen Kate as his mate.

And she had rejected him.

He should be torn apart with sadness. He would never know human happiness now, never click into his human form for good.

Dr. Bhimani had explained to him that humans could lose a lover and find happiness again one day. But he knew instinctively that this wasn't true for his race. Kirk and his brothers had a single choice, a single chance.

His only hope now was that Kate might change her mind.

Though it was hard for him to wish for that, if he used his head instead of his heart.

She was right - if it came out that he was an alien, things would go badly for everyone back at the lab in Stargazer.

And beyond that, if being mated to him meant she had to abandon her own dreams, then he was willing to live with this sadness and let her go.

He hoped that if he made himself useful to the gentle inhabitants of this planet, he could have a worthwhile life, even if it was a lonely one.

Assuming his other brothers were successful enough to convince the rulers of Aerie that the Earth was worth keeping intact.

The downside now was that while he had felt useful guarding Kate, he was completely useless at Cecily's booth. He could see how Solo had been a help setting up all the various items that were heavy and too high for her to reach, but at this point she could handle everything herself.

"Hey, Kirk," Cecily said, handing him a white paper bag. "There's a turkey sandwich in there and a Coke."

"Thank you, Cecily," Kirk said politely. "Do you need my help this afternoon?"

"Not really," she admitted. "Though my fans definitely appreciate your company."

Kirk laughed.

"No, I'm fine," she said. "Go explore the Con or do whatever you want. Let me know if you need anything."

"Thank you, Cecily," he said. "I'll check in with you in a while in case you need me later."

He waved to her and headed out, bag in hand, to check in on Kate.

Her line was closed, as he had expected. She was likely on her lunch break too.

He headed out the paneled door and down the hallway to the green room.

Light streamed in the windows and he caught his breath at the beauty of the city skyline. It filled him with wonder to think that in each room of all those buildings were people, minds filled with the complicated beauty and pain of life on this mysterious planet.

When he reached the green room door he took a deep breath, then knocked.

"Who is it?" Solo's authoritative voice asked at once.

"Kirk," Kirk replied.

"Ah, come in, brother," Solo opened the door.

Kate looked up from her phone.

"Hi Kate," Kirk said. "I thought maybe we could share some lunch?"

He held up the bag.

"I have already brought her eight sandwiches, brother," Solo said proudly, gesturing to the counter, where indeed, an impressive number of sandwiches were lined up, unopened.

"We can still chat," Kate said quickly, slipping the phone back into her pocket.

"I'll just run a quick errand," Solo said. "I'll be back at the end of your break."

Kate smiled and Kirk felt his heart melt.

Solo slipped out, closing the door quietly behind him.

"I don't mean to intrude," Kirk said. "I just wanted to talk with you now that we are both feeling less surprised."

"I'm sorry I reacted like that," Kate said. "I don't blame you. You've been so quick to help. I was just upset."

Kirk pulled up a chair and sat.

"You were right to be upset," he told her. "I didn't know how important your position was. I mean, I knew that you were an actress, but that doesn't exist on my planet. And fame is something I'm only beginning to wrap my understanding around."

"It's pretty weird, right?" Kate asked. "I still can't get it straight in my own head sometimes."

"The reason I wished to talk with you is that I wanted you to know that I understand why you don't want to be with me," he told her, determined to say what he had come here to say even though all he wanted to do was throw himself at her feet. "Our relationship would be a danger to both my family and your career. And I won't risk your happiness or theirs to satisfy my own. It feels like I can't live without you, Kate, but I am going to try."

She nodded slowly and he thought for a moment she looked disappointed. But he understood so little of human emotion that he plowed on rather than dwelling on it.

"Cecily is doing very well at her booth and I don't think she needs my help," he said. "I'd like to do something useful. I know when we met you had thought you might be able to help me get a job. Would you still be willing to do that?"

"Actually, I do know a guy at one of the booths who's short-handed today," she said. "Do you think you could help him out? It's not exactly a career move, but if you're wanting to be useful..."

"I would be glad to help," Kirk said, hopping up. "Which booth and what does he need me to do?"

21

KATE

Kate had just enough time to introduce Kirk to the guy at the What-Would-You-Look-Like-As-An-Alien? booth before heading back to her own line.

Solo took his place against the back wall as the first set of fans approached her, giggling.

"Hi, ladies," she said, smiling at them.

"We are *such big fans*," the braver of the two said to her.

"Thank you," Kate replied. "It was an honor to be on the show."

"We are fans of you personally too," the other girl said. "We heard that creeper who played Prazgar was giving you trouble. We think it's awesome that you came to the Con anyway."

"Wow, guys, thanks," Kate said.

"And the hot bodyguards you brought are just the icing on the cake," the first girl said, then erupted in a fit of giggles.

Kate spun around to see how Solo was taking this assault of flirtation.

He stood tall in his bodyguard position but his lips were curving up slightly. She was glad he had a sense of humor about it, and hoped he didn't feel too much like a piece of meat on display.

"Thank you for coming, girls," she said, pushing two signed headshots to them.

They scurried away, and she felt a warmth in her chest at the idea that they had known she was being harassed, and had seen her refuse to give in or back down. As much as she was lauded for being a role model on the show, for the very first time she was surprised to actually *feel* like one in real life.

She threw herself into the rest of the meet and greets until her line finally dwindled to nothing.

Solo walked her down the hallway, where she popped into the green room and donned her disguise.

She emerged to find Solo sitting on one of the chairs, gazing at himself in the mirror with the look of a scientist studying a Petri dish.

"Everything okay?" she asked him.

"Yes, of course," he said, turning to her.

"Is it weird to have a human body?" she asked.

"Yes," he admitted. "And even more strange to know that women find it attractive."

"Not that strange," Kate said with a wink.

"Cecily doesn't think so," Solo said wistfully.

"What?" Kate asked.

"She hasn't said as much," Solo explained. "But she isn't attracted to me."

"Why would you think that?" Kate asked.

"I asked her to be my mate, and she said no," he said plainly.

"You did?" Kate was astounded.

"Oh yes," Solo said. "I knew immediately, before I even laid eyes on her."

"How could you know *before* you laid eyes on her?" Kate demanded.

Solo looked suddenly taken aback.

"That was a figure of speech," he said quickly. "But what I mean to say is that I knew right away."

"Humans don't normally make a big commitment without getting to know each other first," Kate explained. "You need to give her time."

Solo nodded, but he didn't look convinced.

"She likes you," Kate confided. "I'm sure of it. Just be patient."

"Thank you, Kate," Solo said. "I will be patient."

He sat back in his chair, looking greatly relieved.

"I'm going to explore the Con a bit," Kate said. "I don't need a bodyguard since I'm in my disguise, but you're welcome to join me."

"I think I'll stick around here a while," Solo said. "I want to do some reading."

Kate tried to hide her smile as he pulled a copy of Cecily's autobiography, *Make-up Sex*, out of his pocket.

"See you later," she told him, and set off, her spirits still high from the meet and greet.

Half an hour later, all her good feelings were fleeing like rats from a sinking ship.

She stood at a t-shirt booth that looked out over four aisles of the Con. Down one of them was the What-Would-You-Look-Like-as-an-Alien? booth.

Kirk leaned back casually against the counter, surrounded by a semi-circle of preening women. The proprietor had clearly assigned him to work the crowd once he saw how people were reacting to him.

The owner was taking handfuls of cash as fast as he could as Kirk smiled at the women and led them one at a time to the photo booth.

Kate cringed as one of them stroked his biceps on her way to the booth.

He's just doing his job. And you don't want to be with him anyway, Kate's inner coach told her sternly.

But it was impossible to look away.

And she had the sick feeling inside that although she was trying to protect her dreams, she was really just watching them fizzle.

Kirk had thought she was awfully special. But at this rate it would be no time at all before he found another condo to crash in and another woman to put on a pedestal.

22

SPENCER

Spencer Carson wandered the Convention Hall aimlessly.

He'd arrived early, but when he learned that Katie's signings didn't begin until late morning he went to the cafe downstairs and had a good breakfast and a couple of energy drinks before heading back up.

He was surprised not to have heard from her after she received his gift. He'd waited up late, sure that he would get a phone call. She would go on and on pretending that she didn't want him in her home or that she wanted him to leave her alone, secretly getting off on the excuse to talk to him.

But she hadn't called. She hadn't even texted. And she hadn't called the police, as far as he knew.

What *had* she done?

There were a million possible scenarios.

He might have enjoyed thinking about them if the private investigator hadn't told him the big goofy bodyguard had spent the night.

That narrowed it down to only a few scenarios.

And none of them involved Katie stripping off her

clothes and rolling around naked in Spencer's roses, fantasizing that it was him all over her body.

A lesser man might have thought that his attentions had pushed the bodyguard into her bed.

But Spencer Carson knew better.

This was just one more way for the little whore to play hard to get. Nothing got her off more than torturing him and pretending not to care.

Well, two could play at that game.

He stayed away from the *Suspended in Space* table and instead wandered the hall, looking for someone to flaunt in front of her.

There were plenty of Katie Bly cosplayers, but they were all cows up close compared to the real thing. Besides, that wouldn't feel like ignoring her. That would be the opposite. He needed to let her know she was the last thing on his mind. He racked his brain for a way to make that clear.

He found a pretty hot Wonder Woman, but she spurned his advances. She was probably a lesbian. Spencer was pretty sure that when you put that many women on an island without men the writing was on the wall, so he didn't take it personally.

He was rounding a corner in hot pursuit of a serviceable Harley Quinn when he saw something interesting.

The bodyguard, Kate's freaking bodyguard, was leaning on the counter of one of the booths, women fawning all over him.

The guy ignored the flirtation, like he was a teacher or a cop or something, which only increased Spencer's irritation.

But he stayed anyway to watch the guy for a minute. It would be good to get in his head, figure him out. Hell, maybe Spencer could even get to the bottom of what the brute had done to him last time they crossed paths.

No matter how many times he went over it in his head, Spencer just couldn't see how the bodyguard had lifted him up so easily. Clearly he was a big dude, but so was Spencer. It just didn't seem possible.

And then there was that business of not being able to move afterward. It was just... impossible.

The clues had to be here though.

Spencer examined the man from afar.

He was very tall, dark hair, gray eyes. He wasn't wearing any kind of patches or pins that would indicate he was into martial arts.

He was super good-looking, almost suspiciously so. He looked more like he was a model or a soap star, not a bodyguard.

Spencer's eye kept getting drawn to the sign over the guy's head. He was at that dumb What-Would-You-Look-Like-As-An-Alien? booth, and he was standing directly under the third panel of the sign, so there were giant letters over his head that said:

An ALIEN?

It was super distracting. Spencer wished the guy would walk away from it so he could stop accidentally reading the sign every time he tried to figure out what was up with the dude.

Stop, Spencer, he told himself. *Think.*

Those were the words his impulse control coach had taught him to repeat to himself whenever he got rammy. The guy was a real nut-job. His mom had hired him, and almost nothing he said made a bit of sense to Spencer. But the stop-think advice was handy now and then.

Spencer stopped and looked at the bodyguard and tried to think clearly.

His eyes went back to the sign.

An ALIEN?

He wrenched his eyes back to the man.

The man was enormous, unusually attractive, and had some kind of weird fighting skills...

An ALIEN?

Something incredible occurred to Spencer.

This guy looked *a lot* like those big dudes from another planet that had been all over the news lately.

Spencer was pretty sure the whole thing was a hoax, but the rest of the world seemed to think it was legit.

He looked back at the guy, assessing him.

Maybe he had used crazy alien superpowers in their fight. That was the only way to explain him getting the best of someone as experienced as Spencer.

His heart began to pound with excitement. He had figured it out, for sure. And without any outside help.

He spun on his heel and half-jogged out of the crowded hall. He needed to get somewhere where it wasn't so crowded. Then he'd be able to think.

He headed up the first set of stairs he found.

He had made an unbelievable discovery. That much was for sure.

And having this piece of secret information would definitely be advantageous to him.

It was only a matter of how advantageous.

He found himself in a quiet space, where a baby grand piano sat overlooking the west entrance and the lobby below. He approached the piano bench and sat. On TV, smart characters sometimes played music to help them think. Spencer couldn't play any instruments. But the view was nice.

He was watching the people milling about in the lobby below when the real truth of the situation hit him.

Katie was seeing an alien. She was sleeping with a real, godforsaken alien.

And it wasn't Prazgar.

Spencer took a deep breath and willed himself not to let the rage consume him.

Stop. Think.

He wondered why the alien was pretending not to be an alien. If Spencer were an alien, he'd be strutting his stuff for the press. But these aliens were kind of private, from what he'd been able to pick up.

As a matter of fact, it occurred to him that according to GQ, there were only three aliens on Earth in the first place. And they were in some dinky little rural town. They weren't supposed to be in the city.

And they had all gotten married, so one of them definitely shouldn't be sleeping with Katie Henderson.

Spencer was so thunderstruck he froze in place, causing a woman behind him to smash into his back and spray him with some kind of coffee concoction.

"Oh geez, I'm so sorry," she quavered.

"Watch it, loser," he roared. "I'm trying to think."

She scurried away as he tried to wipe the whipped cream off his shirt.

So Katie was sleeping with an alien and keeping it a secret because he was married to someone else.

That was information he could use.

As far as Spencer saw it, the info could help him in one of two ways. Either he could tell Kate that he knew everything and use that leverage to get what he wanted from her...

Or he could blow the doors off the thing in revenge, and watch from the sidelines as it all blew up in her face.

Then, when her chips were down, Spencer would have the pleasure of swooping in to pick up the pieces of her broken life.

Like taking candy from a baby.

23

SPENCER

A few hours later, Spencer sat in the lower level cafe, putting the final touches on his epic plan.

His fingers clacked on the keys of his laptop and his blood sizzled with anticipation and the zing of the energy drink he'd just pounded.

Everything would have been perfect if the woman sitting across from him could have kept her toddler under control.

The kid had two tiny pigtails, though she had barely enough wispy curls to need pinning up as far as Spencer could see. A thick bead of yellow snot peeked out of her left nostril periodically before being snorted back up. Her t-shirt said *Future Leader*. Spencer wasn't so sure about that.

"Who are *you*?" she demanded in a voice pitched so high Spencer figured it would give a dog a headache.

He decided it was best to ignore her.

"Who are you?" she asked again, coming closer. Maybe she thought he hadn't heard her crystal-shattering question the first time.

"I'm working, kid," he told her.

"I'm Maddie," she squeaked, undeterred. "Who are *you*?"

"Do you mind?" Spencer called to the girl's mother.

The woman glanced up from her phone. Her face looked like she hadn't slept in a year.

"Maddie," she called tiredly. "Come back here."

"Who are you?" Maddie asked quickly, as if knowing the gig was almost up.

"I'm Spencer fucking Carson," he roared. "Leave me alone."

The mother ran over, snatched the kid under her armpits, and hoisted her up.

"His middle name is a real bad word, Mommy," the girl whispered as she was whisked away.

Spencer laughed.

"Future leader, my ass."

He went back to his work, put the finishing touches on his email and then sat back to read it over.

Your competitor published pictures this morning making it look like Katie Henderson is dating her bodyguard.

But did you know that he's an alien?

Come to the Philadelphia Convention Center west entrance at 7:15pm tonight and I promise you a scoop that will have your readers crapping their pants.

- A friend

Yes, it was perfect. Precise, professional, and it included just enough info to make them all show up.

He copied the text and carefully visited as many news

and gossip sites as he could, emailing it to their news tip inboxes.

All he really needed was for one of them to catch it on video but the more that were there the more Katie would be humiliated.

The thought of her big, frightened eyes gleaming in the flash of the cameras had his cock throbbing, so he tried to think about his trap instead.

The witnesses were lined up now. He had taken care of that part of it nicely.

He slipped his cell phone out of his pocket and sent a message to Cecily. He'd gotten her number from one of his dad's producer friends a couple of months ago when he found out she and Katie were friends. She had told him not to text her anymore about Katie, but she would love this message.

SPENCER:

Hey Cecily. I was up all night thinking about my behavior with Katie and I feel really bad. I didn't want to bother her in front of anyone today and I don't want to text her since she asked me not to. But I have something of hers I want to give back to her as well as an apology. I'd like to meet her at 7:15pm at the west entrance for like two minutes. She can bring her bodyguard with her so she won't have to worry that I will ask anything more than the opportunity to tell her I'm sorry and get some closure, for both of us. Would you please tell her?

HE WAITED a few minutes and at last the phone buzzed again.

CECILY:

I'll mention this to her. No promises.

SHIT.

SPENCER:

I'm leaving town tonight, so this is kind of my last opportunity.

CECILY:

Why don't you write her a letter and drop it off with her stuff at my booth?

SPENCER:

I need to apologize in person and can't give this thing to anyone but Katie. Please stop breaking my balls. Just make sure she's there.

THERE WAS NO RESPONSE, but he was pretty sure that meant he'd won.

Women loved apologizing men. Katie would be there all right, with her bodyguard and all her friends too. She would be hoping to get her rocks off by humiliating him in front of everyone.

Well she was in for quite the surprise.

Now he just had to get upstairs and figure out how to deliver the bait.

24

KIRK

Kirk stood in the green room at the end of the day's activities, only a few feet away from Kate as she discussed matters with her roommates.

The short distance between his body and hers pulled at him like the Earth's gravity. It was almost too cruel to have been so close to her and now be banished from her side.

"You don't have to do this," Cecily said to Kate.

"Spencer wants to apologize," Kate said evenly. "If he's ready for closure, so am I. And if he's after something else, Kirk will be with me."

"I thought I was your bodyguard," Solo said.

"I want Kirk for this," Kate said.

Kirk's heart expanded in his chest and he managed to catch her eye.

She smiled at him and there was sadness in her eyes, though he had done everything she asked.

"It would be my privilege," he told her.

"So we'll head out there and if anything goes wrong I'll text you guys right away," Kate said.

"No way," Beatrix said. "We're all coming with you."

"You want to watch him apologize?" Kate asked.

"Seriously?" Beatrix asked, shaking her head.

Cecily elbowed Bea in the ribs.

"You don't really think he's going to apologize do you?" Bea asked Cecily.

"He owes her an apology. But what does he have that's yours?" Cecily asked Kate.

Kate got an uncomfortable look on her face.

It suddenly occurred to Kirk that they had been so hypnotized by each other and then so shocked by the photographs that Kate had never told everyone about last night.

He could tell by Kate's expression that she was worried about telling them.

"He was in the apartment last night," she said slowly. "He could have taken something then."

"You let him come over?" Cecily asked.

"I told you we should have made them go to the party with us," Bea said.

"I didn't let him come over," Kate said. "He came in on his own and he was gone by the time Kirk and I got there. He left flowers in my bed."

"He *broke* in?" Cecily asked.

Kate nodded.

"Did you call the police?" Cecily asked.

Kate shook her head.

"I didn't want to get the guys in hot water. And I planned to talk to building security today. I would have told you guys if our morning hadn't been so... unusual."

"It isn't safe for you to meet with him, Kate," Cecily said. "He's already demonstrated that he doesn't respect boundaries."

"What do you think he took?" Bea asked.

"I'm not sure," Kate admitted. "And you're right, I wouldn't meet him if not for the fact that this is in public. And if there's any chance that I can get him off my back, I couldn't live with myself if I didn't try. You said he's leaving town, right?"

Cecily nodded slowly.

"We will all come with you, Kate," Solo said. "Not just Kirk and your friends. Buck and I will be there too."

"It's 7:13," Bea said.

Cecily shook her head.

"I'm doing this," Kate said.

Kirk headed out by her side, placing one protective hand between her shoulder blades.

He glanced behind him and was glad to see that the entire group was following, even Cecily, though she did not look pleased.

They headed down the hallway, out past the incoming security checkpoint and down the elevators.

Though he was very concerned for Kate's safety, Kirk trusted her judgment. He felt a cool calm settle around him as they walked.

He was prepared to do whatever it took to protect her. If the man tried to touch her, Kirk would put a quick stop to it.

They reached the metal exit door to the west entrance.

Kirk stepped in front of Kate to push it open.

The sun was setting, its flames reflecting madly against the glass of the surrounding buildings. It took a moment for his eyes to adjust.

People were gathered on the sidewalk below the stairs, dozens of them. They were all standing and facing the building as if Kirk and his friends were putting on a play.

He scanned the crowd for Spencer as he descended the stairs from the Convention Center, but didn't see him.

By the time he realized that Spencer really wasn't there, the whole group was on the steps.

He turned back to Kate to tell her, and then he saw it.

Glass was exploding out of the window over her head.

Something massive tilted and began to fall with the twinkling shards.

Kirk saw its trajectory and his blood went cold.

He had less than a second to decide - his mate's safety or his own.

But there was no decision to be made, not really.

He was already closing his eyes, reaching his consciousness out to envelope the big thing and the glass, releasing it from the reach of the law that pulled it downward…

25

KATE

Kate arrived on the steps just in time to hear a terrific crash from above.

She looked up to find the source, but what she saw didn't seem real.

A storm of shattered glass fell toward her upturned face.

A baby grand piano tilted downward to follow it.

There was no time to move - no time to even think.

Kate barely managed to close her eyes before impact.

But nothing touched her. She'd heard about the sensation that time slowed down during a crisis, but had never experienced anything like this.

The gasp from the crowd at the bottom of the stairs made her open her eyes.

The piano was frozen, hovering a foot from her head.

The glass shimmered, motionless in the air around her.

"Move away, Kate," Buck said, offering her his hand.

She allowed herself to be dragged to the side of the steps.

Kirk stood beside her, eyes closed.

"It's okay now," Buck whispered to him.

Kirk's eyes opened and there was a melodious crash as the piano fell the last six feet from the air to the stairs and the glass rained down around it.

"Did you... did you stop that from hitting me?" Kate whispered to him.

He nodded, eyes wide.

"I'm sorry. There was no other way to save you."

Kate's mind was a whirlwind.

There were people below, so many people, and they had all seen it. Kirk would be in danger now, all his brothers, Rima...

Unless...

She had a decision to make.

But she was already stepping forward, smiling and clapping her hands.

There was no decision, not really.

"Ladies and gentleman," she called to the onlookers. "I hope we didn't scare you too much. We owe the scene you just witnessed to the amazing special effects of Cecily Page and friends."

Cecily took the hint and gave a little bow and a wink.

"The point of this little stunt was to let you all know that Beatrix Li's graphic novel, *Door to Everywhere*, is going to be made into a movie."

A murmur went through the crowd.

Kate started to recognize more faces. These were all reporters and bloggers. And they were the same journalists who had been writing stories about Kate not taking on any film roles.

She had no idea what they were doing there. But she knew the one thing that would make them forget all about the piano.

"And I will be starring in it," she added.

Chew on that.

She glanced over at Beatrix, who observed her with her eyebrows lifted in question.

Kate grinned at her and nodded.

Bea's face blossomed into a genuine, happy smile.

Kate felt good helping so many friends at once. She had saved the aliens, and Beatrix would get to make her movie.

"Bea is going to answer your questions about the film now," Kate said. "I hope you'll all be sure to come out and support it. It's going to be epic."

Bea gave Kate a dirty look. She wasn't much for public speaking, but Kate figured it was high time for her to come out of her shell.

Buck walked over to stand by Bea's side and Kate smiled at the look of relief Bea shot his way.

"You're amazing," Kirk breathed to her as he walked her back into the building. "You saved me."

"I think you have it backwards," Kate said. "What did you do out there?"

"I have a... gift," he told her. "All my brothers do. We each have a sort of superhuman power. We think it's the byproduct of our strengths from back on Aerie."

"So you can move things with your mind?" she asked.

"Not exactly," he said. "I can manipulate the way an object's mass interacts with fundamental physical forces exerted by other aggregations of matter."

She gave him a dubious look.

"I can control gravity," he said.

"You can control gravity?" she echoed helplessly.

"When the object is nearby," he said. "And only for a short time."

Kate tried to imagine having such a power and couldn't.

It was completely unbelievable. Except for the fact that she had literally just witnessed it in action.

"I used it in the confrontation with Spencer last night," Kirk admitted. "I had hoped he hadn't picked up on it, but I think he figured it out."

"So he wasn't actually trying to kill me with that piano," Kate said. "He was trying to get you to show yourself as an alien."

That explained the gaggle of reporters.

"We don't know that it was him," Kirk pointed out.

"Who else would push a piano out a window onto my head?" Kate asked.

"Will the police catch him?" Kirk asked.

"The Convention Center is full of security cameras," Kate said. "I'm sure one of them caught this. But since we said it was a publicity stunt, they won't really be looking."

"Who will pay for the damages?" Kirk asked.

"I'll text Carol to have it taken care of," Kate said. "Times like this, it's nice to have TV star money. I'm just glad no one was hurt."

"Television stars make a lot of money?" Kirk asked.

"Yes," Kate said. "I'm not a billionaire or anything, but I can handle replacing a piano and a plate glass window."

"Are you really going to be in your friend's movie?" Kirk asked.

Kate nodded.

"But you don't want to be known for outer space movies," Kirk said sadly. "You want to make a difference in the world."

"You're a good listener, did you know that?" Kate asked.

A smile lit up his handsome face.

"I've learned a lot about myself and what's important to me this weekend," she said slowly. "And I think I can actually make a difference as Katie. I might rather be Kate in my real life, but Katie has influence in ways Kate never could. I'm going to embrace that instead of fighting it. I *like* being Katie sometimes."

Kirk smiled and nodded.

"But you already saw that in me, didn't you?" she asked.

"I see so much in you, Kate," he said, stopping to take her hands. "I know you've changed your mind about some things today. I hope that I might be one of them."

She looked up into his handsome face, losing herself in those cool gray eyes.

She had known him for such a short time, yet he had shown her so much of himself. He had shown her parts of herself, too. Was it really so strange that she felt she had known him for an eternity?

She looked up at him, unsure what to say.

"I chose you as my mate the day we met," he told her. "You do not have to answer me now. But I want you to know that my heart is yours if you ever decide to accept it."

"A mate is forever," she said.

"Yes," he told her solemnly.

Instead of feeling the heavy burden of the decision, she felt a sudden lightness in her heart.

"Are you doing something to me?" she asked.

"What do you mean?"

"Are you... messing with my gravity?" she asked.

"No," he said, looking mystified. "Why? Is there something wrong with it?"

"More like something right," she said with a smile. "My answer is yes. I accept you as my mate."

He bent to kiss her and, she finally understood what people meant when they talked about time slowing down.

Kirk's mouth was warm against hers.

She went up on her toes to put her arms around his neck.

He wrapped his arms around her, one hand spreading wide between her shoulder blades, pressing her closer.

Kate was lost in his embrace, waves of desire pounding through her body as he kissed her carefully, thoroughly.

"Um, hey, guys," Beatrix's voice seemed to come from far away.

Kate managed to pull away from Kirk.

"Hi," Kate said, running a hand through her hair as she turned to her friends.

Beatrix stood before her with Buck at her side. Cecily and Solo were behind them.

"Thank you so much," Bea said. "You don't have to actually do the movie."

"Oh, I can't wait to do the movie," Kate said. "I mean, if you want me for it. I'll play any part you want. I could do a cameo if you have someone else in mind for the lead."

"Are you kidding?" Bea asked. "If you're willing to do it, I'd kill to have you as the lead. But... you know I can only pay you SAG minimum, right?"

"I knew that," Kate said. "And I'm fine with it. I'm really excited to work with you, Bea."

"Me too," Bea smiled.

"We're going to get something to eat," Cecily said. "Want to join us?"

"I um, I think Kirk and I want to go home and talk," Kate said.

"Talk, huh?" Bea teased.

Cecily elbowed her in the ribs.

"If you keep elbowing me, I'm going to take a self defense class," Bea muttered.

"See you guys at home later," Cecily said. "And great job,

Kirk. I'm glad Kate has someone to look out for her since she's clearly hell bent on putting herself in harm's way."

Kate watched as the four of them headed down the hallway toward the north exit.

Just then, there was a commotion as two security guards dragged someone down the hall.

Kate turned to see Spencer Carson trying to break free.

"Gentlemen," she said to the guards, turning on the charm. "You can let him go. He only did it as part of a publicity stunt."

"We weren't informed of any publicity stunt," one of the guards said.

"I'm very sorry," Kate told him. "We made this plan at the last minute, and didn't think it through, or of course we would have made sure you were informed. My manager has all the necessary permits from the convention center," she lied. "I'll be sure to ask that you be compensated for your trouble."

"He hasn't been cooperative," the other guard said. "We're going to escort him out of the building regardless."

"That's fine," Kate said. "Would you mind giving me a moment with him first?"

The first guard shrugged.

"Sure, Katie," the second one grinned. A fan. Thank goodness for small favors.

They let go of Spencer, who shook himself like a golden retriever who had been yanked out of the pool.

The guards backed off a bit, giving Kate room to talk to Spencer.

"A publicity stunt?" Spencer spat.

"Careful," Kirk said coolly.

"You're lucky you're not going to jail," Kate told Spencer. "Now here's what's going to happen. You're going to be polite to those guards, you're going to leave, and if I catch you at any Con I attend in the future, I'm going to tell the truth about what happened, and I'll have copies of the security footage to back me up. Do I make myself understood?"

Spencer scowled at her, but nodded.

"Good," Kate said, turning on her heel.

She gestured to the guards and they jogged up to retrieve Spencer immediately.

Kate turned back to watch as they led him outside.

He looked smaller somehow. She hoped he would remember their arrangement.

"Whether he honors that agreement or not, you have me now," Kirk said, echoing her thoughts. "It just means I can't let you out of my sight."

"Good thing I don't want you to." Kate smiled up at him.

"Let's go home," Kirk said, his voice husky.

26

KIRK

Kirk stood in Kate's room.

It seemed that she had been in the shower for hours, though the clock told him it had only been minutes since they'd returned home.

He paced the floor like a tiger, trying not to let himself get nervous. It was important that tonight be special, that he sweep her off her feet.

He caught sight of his own reflection in the mirror over her dresser and stopped to peel his t-shirt over his head, remembering how she had reacted to the sight of his bare chest.

The man staring back at him in the mirror looked human - larger and more chiseled than most, but human. Soon, Kirk would be truly human.

When his brothers back in Stargazer first told him of the *click,* it had frightened him to think of being trapped in this form forever.

But now it felt right. Everything felt right when Kate was near.

The sound of her footsteps in the hallway roused him from his thoughts.

She opened the door and he stared at her, unabashed. Her curving figure was silhouetted in the light from the hallway. She had wrapped a towel around her breasts like a tiny dress.

"Hi," she said softly.

"Hi," he replied, loving her sudden shyness. "Come here."

She padded over slowly and stood before him, gazing up with those luminous brown eyes.

He reached out and slipped his finger into the place where her towel was tucked.

Kate's breath caught, but she didn't protest. Her eyes danced.

He swept the towel off her like a matador and flung it to the ground.

She giggled.

"This is no time for giggling, woman," he told her. "We are joining for life. This is serious business."

"Life is not serious business," she informed him. "Life is wild and ridiculous. Haven't you learned anything from the time you've spent with me?"

He bent to kiss her smiling lips.

Her mouth was minty and delicious. She kissed him back like she meant it.

His whole body surged with lust. He closed his eyes, willing himself to slow down, to please her first.

Kate pressed herself closer, her bare breasts flattening against his chest.

Kirk groaned and pulled back.

She looked up at him with glittering eyes.

Oh, how he loved her unapologetic need. Earth women

in movies were so demure. They needed saving, They pretended not to want to be held and kissed.

But this woman of his would drive him to distraction.

"Lean back," he told her.

Her eyes widened slightly, but she did as she was told and leaned back against the dresser, the position thrusting her hips forward.

He prayed by the moons of Aerie for the strength to be patient.

Kate watched him, her lips parted slightly.

Kirk placed his hands on her waist and knelt before her, pressing his face to her belly.

She gasped in surprise, but didn't wiggle away.

He kissed his way down to her hip, licking away stray droplets of water on his way.

By the time he reached her thighs, she was trembling.

"Slide your feet apart," he told her.

She obeyed and he nearly groaned at the sight of her pink sex glistening just inches from his hungry mouth.

Her thighs tensed with anticipation.

He leaned forward leisurely and pressed a kiss to her tender opening.

Kate moaned lightly and he heard her nails click against the dresser.

He smiled and pressed his mouth to her again, licking a slow line upward through the sweet spiciness of her.

She moaned again.

He slid a finger inside her, his cock throbbing at the wet heat of her.

Kate whimpered.

"Easy," he whispered to her.

He licked her again, moving his finger slowly.

Her sounds were like music.

Kirk spread her folds with his other hand to allow his tongue better access to her stiff little clit.

She cried out and thrust her hips out slightly as if begging for more, so he gave it to her, stroking her lovingly with his tongue as he slid his finger in and out of her velvet depths.

"Ohhh," she moaned.

He pulled back, slowing his movements just enough to delay her climax.

Kate shivered.

He applied himself to her once again, lapping at her and working her with his hand until she was panting with need, her thighs stiffening.

Again he slowed his pace.

"Please," Kate moaned brokenly.

He would have liked to have teased her all night, brought her closer and closer.

But his own body was humming with need and his heart ached to claim her. There would be other nights for games.

"Let me take care of you properly," he whispered to her, standing and leading her to the bed, their bed.

She crawled in and lay on her back, arms open to Kirk. Her cheeks were flushed pink. She had never been more beautiful to him.

But that would always be true.

He blinked, and a succession of images of Kate throughout her life flashed before his eyes. One had a pregnant belly, one had lines under her eyes, and one lay back against the bed, her long, silver hair spread out against the pillow.

All were the most beautiful. And each was more beloved than the last.

27

KATE

Kate lay back in the bed, breathless with need.

Kirk stood over her, magnificent in the moonlight that streamed in from the window.

"Are you ready?" he asked.

She felt for a moment as if she were the alien, her mind unable to comprehend any language in the face of the relentless demands of her body.

The words arranged themselves in her head at last. He was going to make love to her.

She nodded, not trusting herself to speak.

He smiled down, those steel gray eyes warm and kind.

He crawled on top of her, caging her head between his arms, and pressed his forehead to hers.

"I love you, Kate," he told her. "I will always love you."

"I love you too," she whispered.

He kissed her slowly, carefully. She would never get used to such patient kisses.

But she could feel his cock, desperately hard and throbbing against her belly. Surely he couldn't make her wait forever.

Then he was sliding a hand down the curve of her hip, lifting her leg to wrap it around his waist.

Kate felt suddenly nervous. It wasn't like she'd never done this before. But it had never been like this - never felt like it was the most important thing that would ever happen to her.

Kirk lifted himself slightly from her, using his hand to guide himself against her opening.

She whimpered with the pleasure that licked her insides at the place where the tip of him touched her.

He kissed her again and she jogged her hips upward, begging wordlessly.

He growled into her mouth and then pressed himself slowly inside her.

"Kate," he groaned.

Kate froze, her hips slightly lifted, and felt her body stretching to accommodate him.

Kirk held still, as if waiting for her discomfort to subside.

The slight pain blossomed into pleasure in a heartbeat and Kate sank her nails into his shoulders, frantic.

He responded instantly, drawing himself out of her slowly, then filling her again.

Kate felt the pleasure building inside her already, thundering closer with every breath.

Kirk nuzzled her neck and plunged inside her again, his movement less controlled.

She moaned as he filled her, jogging her hips up shamelessly, chasing her release.

Kirk brushed her lips with his and slid a hand between them to massage her clitoris as he thrust inside her once more.

Her climax was a tidal wave now. It carried her higher

and higher then broke as the pleasure crashed down on the shore again and again.

Kirk groaned and came with her, filling her as she tightened around him in endless convulsions of ecstasy.

The air seemed to go out of the room for an instant, as if the pressure had dropped.

Then Kate's head fell back against the pillow at last.

"That was incredible," she breathed.

"Kate," Kirk said, kissing her nose, her forehead, her cheeks. "How I love you."

He rolled to his side, so as not to crush her.

It was only then that she noticed something was different.

"Kate," he breathed in wonder.

She looked over at him and saw that a lock of her hair was floating in the air between their faces, as if she were underwater.

"Are you doing that?" she asked.

He shook his head.

Then she realized she wasn't touching the bed anymore.

"Dr. Bhimani explained that this might happen," Kirk said. "Sometimes we are able to share our gifts at the moment of clicking."

Kate gazed at him in wonder as the petals from the flowers they had swept to the floor last night began to lift and swirl around the bed.

"Are you okay with this?" he asked, worry marring his handsome face.

He had changed her life forever, by just being part of it – taken the things that might have once seemed like negatives and turned them into something magical. How could she not be okay with that?

"I love this," she whispered, trying to figure out why this

was so familiar, when it would have been impossible for her to imagine such a moment.

Her happiness was so intense she felt she would float away like a balloon.

Kirk took her hands, squeezing them gently between his, and she felt anchored in spite of her floating body and the swirling rose petals.

Then it hit her.

This was the dream. Some part of her mind had known this was coming, had seen it was her destiny.

"What is it, Kate?" Kirk asked.

"I can't wait to see what comes next," Kate said, pulling gently on his hands to bring herself back to him. She had a lifetime to tell him about the dream. Right now she only wanted to feel him inside her again.

He smiled up at her and she pressed her lips to his in a patient kiss of her own.

28

KATE

Kate must have fallen asleep in his arms after making love for the second time.

She awoke to the sounds of muffled giggling in the hallway.

She lifted her head from Kirk's warm chest.

He made a sleepy sound of protest.

"It's okay," she whispered to him. "The others just got home, I want to say hi. I'll come right back."

"Not without me you won't," he murmured, opening his eyes and trapping her in his hypnotic gray gaze.

A shiver of desire shot down her spine.

"Are you sure you don't want to stay?" he asked, one eyebrow arched.

Kate launched herself out of bed.

Kirk laughed as she wrapped a robe around herself.

He got up and pulled on his jeans while she ran a brush through her hair.

She threw his t-shirt at him.

"You really want me to put this on?" he asked.

"Yes," she said with a grin. "I like watching you take it off."

His gray eyes flashed.

"Friends and food," she reminded him.

He pulled on the shirt and opened the bedroom door and they headed out together.

The giggling in the living room suddenly went quiet.

"Hey guys," Kate called.

"Hey," Cecily said.

The four were piled up on the sectional sofa. The coffee table in front of them held six milkshakes and a white paper bag.

"We brought you some dinner," Bea said.

"We thought you might need to supplement your strength," Solo said.

Buck elbowed him.

"For the mating," Solo qualified. "Why did you elbow me?"

Buck shook his head in wonder as Cecily threw her head back and laughed.

"Thank you," Kate said firmly.

Kirk sat and she opened the paper bag. The contents smelled heavenly.

She pulled out two cheeseburgers in waxed paper and a cardboard tray of sweet potato fries.

"Oh, yes," she moaned, handing a burger to Kirk.

When they were snuggled onto the sofa, food in their laps, shakes in their hands, she looked around.

"So, how was dinner?" Kate asked.

"It was awesome," Bea said. "Non-stop text messages, of course."

"From well-wishers?" Kirk asked politely.

"From well-wishers," Bea agreed. "And from some frenemies pretending to be well-wishers."

"What is a frenemy?" Buck asked.

"An enemy who pretends to be a friend," Beatrix explained.

"I don't understand," Solo said.

"Give it time," Cecily told him, in lieu of explaining.

"Anyway, it was awesome and I'm really excited," Bea said.

"What's the next step?" Kate asked.

"I've got a meeting with the studio in two weeks," Bea explained. "I just have to formalize things with the investors. I've already emailed most of them to let them know that you're on board."

"Great," Kate said. She wasn't about to change her mind. She was excited, really excited, for the first time in a long time.

Bea's phone buzzed.

"There it goes again," Buck said.

"It's okay, it can wait," Bea said.

Kate's phone buzzed.

"Oh gosh, it's probably Carol," Kate said, slamming her palm into her forehead. "I really need to talk to her about our publicity stunt."

She placed her dinner down and slipped her cell phone out of her robe pocket as she headed down the hallway for her room.

It was Carol.

"Hi, Carol," Kate said. "I know I have a lot of explaining to do."

"Not really," Carol said. "I read it all on the gossip sites. Are you really doing this?"

"I am, but don't get excited," Kate said, sitting down on her bed. "It's SAG minimum."

"You know it's not always about the money with me, Kate," Carol said.

Kate felt a stab of guilt. Carol was like a second mother.

"I'm so sorry, that's not what I meant," she said.

"I know, love," Carol said. "But here's the thing, and you're not going to like it. You know Spencer Carson's father was one of the investors for that project, right?"

"I didn't know," Kate said, her heart sinking.

"Well, he is - not under his own name, he's part of a larger angel group but he's the main investor and the decision maker," Carol explained. "He just called me."

Kate waited with bated breath.

"He'll only honor the funding they agreed to if Spencer plays the male lead," Carol said.

"Oh, god," Kate said.

"I told him no way," Carol said immediately.

"Bea really needs the funding," Kate said, wondering if she could tolerate spending time with Spencer if Kirk was nearby.

"She's going to tell him *no* too, if everything I've read about her is accurate," Carol said. "She's probably telling him now. He threatened to call her next if I refused to make you agree."

Katie stuck her head out of her room to hear Bea on the phone already.

"*Absolutely not*," Bea was saying forcefully.

"Yeah, he called," Katie said. "Can I talk with you later?"

"Sure honey," Carol said. "Take care. And remember, Spencer Carson's issues are not your fault or your problem."

"Thanks, Carol," Kate said, hanging up as she headed down the hallway.

"Here's the thing," Bea said. "Even if your demand weren't completely unethical, no one would ever cast him in that role. He's *all wrong* for it."

She nodded, listening.

"Well, good luck with that," she said. "Maybe Spielberg or Tarantino will go for it, but I won't. I'll find my money elsewhere. I'm glad we could clear this up before we got too far."

She paused again and Kate could hear Mr. Carson's screaming through the phone.

"Okay, then, bye-bye now," Beatrix said, hanging up.

She slid the phone back in her pocket and turned to Kate.

"So, we have a funding gap to cover," she said. "No big deal. One of my investors just dropped out. He wanted me to compromise my vision, and I won't play that game."

"I know it was Carson," Kate told her. "Carol just called me."

"Shoot, Kate, I'm sorry," Bea said. "I didn't want you to worry about it."

"It's fine," Kate said, trying to remind herself of Carol's words.

Spencer Carson's issues are not your fault or your problem.

But they were turning out to be Bea's problem and Bea was her friend.

"How much time do we have to find another investor?" Kate asked.

"Two weeks," Bea said, biting her lip.

"Was he putting in a lot?" Kate asked.

"That group was my biggest investor," Bea admitted. "But I didn't have you on board before."

"I'll do whatever I can to help," Kate said. "But I don't

know if my name will bring you as much power as it would have five years ago."

"We'll all do whatever we can," Cecily said, rising from the sofa to put an arm around each of them. "Between us we must know everyone in this industry."

"And you have us," Kirk piped up from his place on the sofa. "We... well, we don't know anything about it. But we will be as helpful as we can."

Beatrix laughed and Kate felt her heart start to beat again.

"Come on, Kate," Bea said. "Sit, eat. We'll worry about this tomorrow. Tonight, let's relax and celebrate."

And although Kate had never been the type to relax when there were things to worry about, she found that it was suddenly easy to sit beside her mate, in the company of her friends, and enjoy a simple meal.

They could solve all their troubles together, she was sure of it.

Tomorrow was a new day.

***

Thanks for reading Kirk!
Keep reading for a sample of the next Stargazer Alien Mail Order Brides book: Buck.

Or grab your next book right now:
http://www.tashablack.com/stargazer.html

BUCK (SAMPLE)

1

BEATRIX

Beatrix Li took a single step down the dark path and felt ice crunch under her foot.

She knew this was a dream, but it felt so real. Her breath misted in the crystalline air. Stars and planets hung low, casting odd shadows against the rocky terrain.

The world was black and white.

And it was framed - a perfect rectangle with only darkness outside the lines - as if she were standing on a stage.

You're just dreaming about the book again, she told herself.

Beatrix had spent enough time drawing and re-drawing the panels of her graphic novel - she certainly recognized the terrain.

She was inside her own comic panel.

But she shouldn't be able to smell the tang of the copper mines in the air, or hear the shimmering song of the frozen lichen moving gently in the breeze.

She turned back, but behind her was only darkness, outside of the frame.

There was no place to go but forward.

She took another step and another, grateful that there

was a path between the crags. Twin boulders stood side by side in the near distance, like a gateway.

But Beatrix didn't know what lay on the other side.

She had never drawn anything beyond the boulders.

She picked up her pace, unaware if safety lay ahead.

A shooting star blitzed across the sky and she stopped to admire its glittering trail. Beatrix loved drawing light and shadow, that was why she had created this world in the first place, and the humans who visited it.

When she looked down again, she saw a flicker of color near the boulders.

She blinked and it disappeared.

Colored panels were expensive to produce, so Beatrix used them sparingly. This world was meant to be black and white.

But as she got closer to the rocks, she saw another flash of purple.

She began to run. Cold air filled her lungs.

When she got closer, she was startled to see a familiar shape.

A butterfly.

The butterfly fluttered closer. Its violet wings were enormous and webbed with delicate turquoise patterns. It sank, then rose with a dainty flap of those impossibly lacy wings.

She had never seen a butterfly in nature with colors like these. Yet it did not belong on this foreign planet, either. It shouldn't have been able to survive the cold.

The butterfly sailed on a current between the boulders, then hung in the air a moment, as if waiting for Beatrix.

She followed.

The world erupted into a riot color as soon as she stepped between the massive rocks.

The icy ground turned pale blue. The cliffs and crags took on the sepia-tones of a Pennsylvania winter.

And the air was filled with the trembling wings of a thousand technicolor butterflies.

Beatrix closed her eyes and counted to seven.

When she opened them again the butterflies were still there.

And a man stood before her.

Tall, dark and handsome didn't begin to describe him. He gazed down at her hungrily.

There was something familiar about his brown eyes and the curve of his sensual mouth.

Beatrix tried to place him, but the air was sizzling between them, pulling her closer.

The man reached out to touch her hair.

Shivers of need ran down her spine at his gentle caress.

He cupped her cheek in his warm hand and leaned down toward her, unhurried.

Every cell in her body thrummed in anticipation. She ached for his touch with a desire so fierce it frightened her.

Somewhere in the distance, bells began to ring.

She tried to ignore them and lose herself in the pull of his big body.

But the sound startled the butterflies and they began to dart away.

"Please," Beatrix murmured, but her plea was lost in the sound of the pealing bells.

And the man whose hand still cradled her cheek was fading away, the warmth of his touch dissipating.

Beatrix awoke with tears prickling her eyes.

Her cell phone cheerfully blasted its alarm on the bedside table, oblivious to the fact that it had shattered the best dream she'd had in a long time.

Beatrix slapped it into submission and flopped back down, rubbing her eyes.

She'd never been a morning person.

And today was moving day.

She and her two roommates, and the three aliens they had taken in, had to pack up their belongings from this rented Philly condo and take a car down to Baltimore for the next leg of the Comic Con circuit.

She ran a hand through her hair and tried to decide whether to get up and get moving early like she had planned, or just snooze for ten minutes.

There was a gentle knock at her door.

"Beatrix?" a deep voice said.

Buck...

The dream flashed back before her eyes and she saw what she hadn't before.

She had been dreaming about Buck.

"Give me a minute," she groaned.

She was exhausted, embarrassed and a little turned on. Definitely not a good combination for seeing Buck face to face.

"You said you wanted to be up early," he said through the door.

"I know, I know, I'm getting up," she told him, suddenly feeling decidedly more awake.

"Okay, I'll see you later," he said, sounding a little amused.

Bea waited until his footsteps told her he was leaving. Then she slid out of bed and wrapped a robe around herself.

She had time for a shower. That was one good thing about being up early.

She grabbed her caddy and headed to the bathroom.

Maybe a good soak under the hot water would get her head in the game. Dreaming about a hunky alien wasn't on her agenda right now.

Beatrix's real dream was on the razor's edge of coming true. She had written a break-out graphic novel that was on every teenager's night stand right now. She had a studio interested in making it into the movie version she'd been envisioning ever since she conceived of the story.

And she finally had a star, her friend and roommate Kate, who would get butts in seats and had the investors interested enough to make the movie happen.

But she'd lost a lot of funding last night.

It was a big price to pay, but her principles were her principles and she would never allow an investor to dictate casting at all - let alone when it came to casting the man who had harassed the star of her film, who also happened to be Bea's friend.

She had two weeks to make up the shortfall.

If Beatrix Li was ever going to be a morning person, now was the time to start.

***

Thanks for reading this sample of Buck!
Grab the rest of the story now:
http://www.tashablack.com/stargazer.html

TASHA BLACK STARTER LIBRARY

Packed with steamy shifters, mischievous magic, billionaire superheroes, and plenty of HEAT, the Tasha Black Starter Library is the perfect way to dive into Tasha's unique brand of Romance with Bite!

Get your FREE books now at TashaBlack.com!

ABOUT THE AUTHOR

Tasha Black lives in a big old Victorian in a tiny college town. She loves reading anything she can get her hands on, writing paranormal romance, and sipping pumpkin spice lattes.

Get all the latest info, and claim your FREE Tasha Black Starter Library at www.TashaBlack.com

Plus you'll get the chance for sneak peeks of upcoming titles and other cool stuff!

Keep in touch...
www.tashablack.com
authortashablack@gmail.com

Lightning Source UK Ltd.
Milton Keynes UK
UKHW04f1854081018
330211UK00001B/30/P